—— .✦. ——

PRAISE FOR DONNA GRANT'S
BEST-SELLING ROMANCE NOVELS

—— .✦. ——

"Grant's ability to quickly convey complicated
backstory makes this jam-packed love story accessible
even to new or periodic readers."
–Publishers' Weekly

"Donna Grant has given the paranormal genre
a burst of fresh air..."
–San Francisco Book Review

"The premise is dramatic and heartbreaking; the characters are
colorful and engaging; the romance is spirited and seductive."
–The Reading Cafe

"The central romance, fueled by a hostage drama, plays
out in glorious detail against a backdrop of multiple ongoing
issues in the "Dark Kings" books. This seemingly penultimate
installment creates a nice segue to a climactic end."
–Library Journal

"...intense romance amid the growing
war between the Dragons and the
Dark Fae is scorching hot."
–Booklist

—— .✦. ——

DON'T MISS THESE OTHER NOVELS BY *NYT & USA TODAY* BESTSELLING AUTHOR DONNA GRANT

—— .✦. ——

CONTEMPORARY PARANORMAL

REAPER SERIES

Dark Alpha's Claim ~ Dark Alpha's Embrace

Dark Alpha's Demand ~ Dark Alpha's Lover

Dark Alpha's Night ~ Dark Alpha's Hunger

Dark Alpha's Awakening ~ Dark Alpha's Redemption

Dark Alpha's Temptation ~ Dark Alpha's Caress

Dark Alpha's Obsession ~ Dark Alpha's Need

Dark Alpha's Silent Night ~ Dark Alpha's Passion

Dark Alpha's Command ~ Dark Alpha's Fury

ELVEN KINGDOMS

Rising Sun

Dark Heart

Storm Wood

Mountain Fire

Burning Sea

THE BASTARD DUOLOGY

The Bastard King

The Uncrowned King

DRAGON KINGS® SERIES

Dragon Revealed ~ Dragon Mine

Dragon Unbound ~ Dragon Eternal

Dragon Lover ~ Dragon Arisen

Dragon Frost ~ Dragon Kiss ~ Dragon Born

Dragon Marked ~ Dragon Forged ~ Dragon Sieged

SKYE DRUIDS SERIES

Iron Ember ~ Shoulder the Skye ~ Heart of Glass

Endless Skye ~ Still of the Night ~ Blood Skye

After Midnight ~ Kiss of Skye

DARK KINGS SERIES

Dark Heat ~ Darkest Flame ~ Fire Rising

Burning Desire ~ Hot Blooded ~ Night's Blaze

Soul Scorched ~ Dragon King ~ Passion Ignites

Smoldering Hunger ~ Smoke and Fire

Dragon Fever ~ Firestorm ~ Blaze ~ Dragon Burn

Constantine: A History, Parts 1-3 ~ Heat ~ Torched

Dragon Night ~ Dragonfire ~ Dragon Claimed

Ignite ~ Fever ~ Dragon Lost ~ Flame ~ Inferno

A Dragon's Tale (Whisky and Wishes: *A Holiday Novella*,

Heart of Gold: *A Valentine's Novella*, and

Of Fire and Flame) ~ My Fiery Valentine

The Dragon King Coloring Book

Dragon King Special Edition

Character Coloring Book: Rhi

DARK SWORD SERIES

Dangerous Highlander

Forbidden Highlander ~ Wicked Highlander

Untamed Highlander ~ Shadow Highlander

Darkest Highlander

ROGUES OF SCOTLAND SERIES

The Craving ~ The Hunger

The Tempted ~ The Seduced

THE SHIELDS SERIES

A Dark Guardian ~ A Kind of Magic

A Dark Seduction ~ A Forbidden Temptation ~ A Warrior's Heart

Mystic Trinity (a series connecting novel)

DRUIDS GLEN SERIES

Highland Mist ~ Highland Nights ~ Highland Dawn

Highland Fires ~ Highland Magic

Mystic Trinity (a series connecting novel)

SISTERS OF MAGIC TRILOGY

Shadow Magic ~ Echoes of Magic ~ Dangerous Magic

THE ROYAL CHRONICLES
NOVELLA SERIES

Prince of Desire ~ Prince of Seduction

Prince of Love ~ Prince of Passion

Mystic Trinity

(a series connecting novel)

Dark Alpha's Hunger

NEW YORK TIMES & USA TODAY BESTSELLING AUTHOR

DONNA GRANT

Dark Alpha's Hunger

THE REAPERS

The seven there are, warriors all.
Do not do wrong or their blade will fall.
Their appearances shrouded.
Their approach, clouded.
Against evil they fight.
Power and magic are their might.
They serve only one.
If you expose their identity – run.
Secrecy is their defense.
If the truth escapes, Death will commence.

Prologue

Twenty-five years ago
Ireland

"Thea! Enough! Get in the vehicle. Now."

She glanced at Mrs. Boyle who ran the children's home. The woman's tone promised retribution, but Thea didn't care. Her attention was drawn back to the portal stones. She felt the vibration of the ancient boulders, and she didn't understand why no one else could.

"Ow," Thea cried when long fingers wrapped painfully around her arm.

Mrs. Boyle jerked her around and put her face near Thea's. "You don't listen, child. And you wonder why others find foster homes and you do not. You've been with us since infancy. In five years, you've yet to grasp that I won't tolerate disobedience."

Even when the thin twig slapped against her bare legs, Thea looked at the stones, her hands yearning to touch them. The wind began to howl. She glanced up to see that the blue sky was gone, replaced by dark, angry clouds. A second later, lightning flashed overhead, quickly followed by thunder that rumbled the ground.

But it didn't scare Thea. All she wanted was to get closer to the boulders. Why wouldn't anyone let her near them? It wasn't as if she could harm them.

She fought against Mrs. Boyle's hold as the headmistress dragged her back to the other children. All the while, Thea kept reaching out to the portal stones.

Long after she was tossed into the vehicle and the door slammed shut, she stared at the ancient boulders until they were no longer in sight. No matter how long it took, she would return.

One day. . . .

CHAPTER

one

Kilkenny, Ireland
February

The portal stones stood against the sunset like giants. And just like many years earlier, they called to her, urging her closer.

Thea's hand tightened on her violin case. It had been nearly three weeks since her last visit to the stones, and each time the same anxiety, the same restlessness filled her. As if her belonging there were preordained.

From the very first time she had seen the megalithic structure, she had been struck by its beauty. And its mystery.

"Leac an Scail," she whispered as she walked closer. Stone of the warrior.

Kilmogue was one of the largest dolmens in all of Ireland. Without a doubt, it was one of the most impressive. It stood twelve feet high with the capstone over thirteen feet long.

Thea reached the stones and set down her case. She rested her hand on one of the boulders and felt the warmth that seemed to radiate out from the inside.

She walked all around the dolmen, looking at the capstone resting on two large boulders with a pillow stone laying on its backstone. She stopped at the entrance that faced northeast with the enormous doorstone almost ten feet high.

For long minutes, she stood in the doorway. Once, about ten years ago, she'd almost gotten the nerve to walk inside. They weren't called portal stones for nothing. But she lacked the courage then. And now.

Instead, she visited the dolmen as often as she could, waiting to see what the stones wanted from her. Because she knew they desired something. Otherwise, why would they continue to call her back?

Thea retrieved her case and gently laid it flat to open it. Then she pulled out the violin and tucked it beneath her chin as she found the bow. She placed her fingers on the strings and closed her eyes to let the music find her. The notes constantly floated around in her mind, forming melodies and songs without any effort. Today was no different.

Placing her bow on the strings, she gently pulled it back, hearing the first soft tones. She gave herself to the music, the notes rising and falling on their own.

And her body played as if controlled by another.

Song after song fell from her hands, filling the air. She lost track of time, as she usually did while playing. But there was nothing purer or more beautiful than music.

It fed her soul as nothing else could. And it had saved her.

At only eight years of age, she had struggled to get through each day. Utterly alone and buried in depression—so low that she actually begged to die while in the children's home. It wasn't death that she was given, but a violin.

Ms. Fylan, who smiled without saying a word, had placed the instrument in Thea's hands. For weeks, Thea sat in music class without attempting to play. Each day, she found herself looking forward to hearing more of the tunes.

Nearly two months passed before she tried to play the violin. From her first cringe-worthy note, she discovered her passion.

While Ms. Fylan had given her the instrument, ultimately, it was the music that saved Thea.

She'd never found a foster family. Instead, she spent her days in the children's home until she was able to go out into the world. Those formative years made her strong enough to survive on her own.

She worked numerous jobs to pay for University. It didn't matter how long her day was or how exhausted she felt, she never went to bed without playing her violin.

That's how Duane found her. He'd been walking home from a gig at a nearby tavern and heard her through an open window. He'd called up to her. While Thea never thought to play in a band, Duane's offer intrigued her.

The next day, she went for an audition, and two nights later, she was performing her first gig. It paid so well that it became her sole source of income.

Returning from her reverie, she finished the last song and let the note fade away. Thea opened her eyes as she lowered her bow arm. Darkness surrounded her, with nothing but the moonlight and stars to light the way.

The inside of the portal stones was black as pitch, but for just a moment, she thought she heard something within. It had been a deep rumbling, almost like a . . . growl.

Thea swallowed, her heart beginning to pound against her chest. She contemplated leaving, but the pull of the stones was too strong.

With the sounds of the night all around her—and nothing coming from the dolmen—she adjusted her chin and began to play again.

Except she kept her eyes open this time. So many times, she'd come to play, but nothing like this had ever happened before. It was a little frightening. Then again, it would take much more than some sound to make her run away.

The way her mood had turned, Thea wasn't surprised when the music shifted from something soft and soothing to a somber, stirring song.

She swayed with the gripping melody. Each note slid through her body until she felt it in every muscle, every bone. She was so engrossed in the music that, at first, she didn't see the glow emanating from within the portal stones.

Thea stepped back and tried to stop playing but she couldn't. The music continued, almost of its own accord. Her gaze was locked on the doorway as the soft pinpoint of light grew larger in diameter.

The edges of the radiance rippled as if it were water. She gasped, her heart jumping into her throat when a hand appeared out of the light.

With fingers spread wide, the appendage reached for something, anything to grab hold of. As more of the arm appeared, she saw the veins protruding and muscles flexing. Almost as if it were taking every bit of strength for whoever was coming through just to pull themselves out.

Suddenly, the arm was yanked back into the darkness until only the wrist and hand remained. Thea set her violin in its case and hesitantly started toward the doorway. She had to turn her head to the side and shield her eyes because the light was so bright.

"What the bloody hell are you doing?" she asked herself.

No one in their right mind would walk toward the scary light and hand. Then again, what kind of sane person played a violin in front of some portal stones?

Thea hesitated another moment before she reached out and grasped the hand. Strong fingers wrapped around hers. The grip was tight and bordered on painful, but she didn't let go. Not even when she was pulled toward the light.

She dug her heels into the earth and used both hands to yank on the appendage. Thea gritted her teeth and used all of her strength to drag the person out —and stop herself from being pulled in.

More of the arm appeared. A moment later, the shoulder. Then a second arm latched onto Thea. That was the only warning she had before she saw the muscles flex in the limbs as the hands yanked.

The heels of her boots sank deeper into the dirt and left trails as she was dragged forward. Somehow, she knew that whoever this was wasn't trying to pull her in. They were attempting to get out. Since there was nothing else for the person to grab onto, she was acting like a rope.

Her eyes widened when a head appeared. Long, inky black hair hung all around the face. Then the chin lifted, and liquid silver eyes speared her.

She found herself staring at a man—a very gorgeous, dirty man.

His face was lined with determination. Suddenly, he looked back into the light and bared his teeth as he growled. But it was the answering rumble of something dark and nefarious that caused her heart to skip a beat.

The man said nothing as he returned his gaze to her. She renewed her efforts while he continued to pull himself out. Finally, he got one leg free and set his foot on the ground. She glanced down and saw that his jeans were in tatters, his limbs coated in blood.

He threw back his head and howled in pain and anger. Thea thought she saw something dark begin to emerge behind him. She barely caught sight of it before the man roughly shoved her away.

It was so unexpected that she stumbled back, trying to get her legs beneath her. Instead, she slammed against one of the portal rocks, knocking the back of her head as she did. Pain exploded, causing her to black out for a second.

She heard grunts but could see little of the fighting because of the bright light. She struggled to get the pain under control so she could see. When she was finally able to focus again, she saw the man hitting what appeared to be a black blob.

Then, he turned and grabbed her. He lifted her in one arm as if she were a sack. Then he tossed her out of the dolmen. She landed hard on her side and rolled. When she stopped, she looked up to find him standing before the portal stones with his legs spread as if he were ready for . . . something.

He had his back to her so she couldn't see his face, but she did glimpse what looked like an iridescent orb that continued to grow bigger and bigger in his hand. Then he threw it at the light.

There was a second of silence before the dolmen exploded. Thea ducked her face and covered her head with her arms. She felt the man land heavily on top of her to shield her from the debris that rained down upon them.

It felt like forever before he rolled off onto his back. Thea glanced at him before she rose up on her elbows to look at him. His quicksilver eyes were locked on her.

She gaped at them and the fact that there were no pupils to be seen. Only pools of beautiful of what looked like liquid mercury.

"Run," he whispered before his eyes closed.

CHAPTER

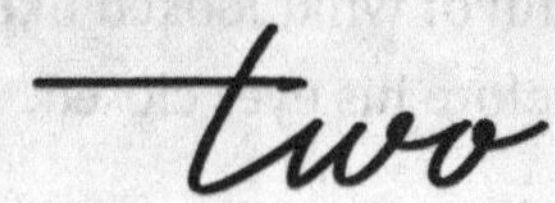

two

The bombardment of his senses slowly pulled Eoghan back to consciousness. He dug his fingers into the chilled grass and dirt. The soft rush of a breeze over his face cooled his flesh and caused a strand of hair to tickle his cheek.

He remained on his back and took it all in. The beast that had chased him was gone, left behind in that horrendous realm of darkness. It was the music that had lured Eoghan to freedom.

His eyes snapped open as he recalled the woman. He stared at the stars above him in the night sky as he remembered how she had pulled him through the doorway. It was by sheer luck that he managed to close the portal before the beast got out.

He sat up and looked around. His gaze clashed with the broken dolmen. There were very few portal stones left intact—and for good reason. They were exactly as they were named. Thanks to a few half-Fae who used what magic they had, mortals had begun crossing into other realms over the centuries.

Most were never seen or heard from again.

Eoghan's thoughts returned to the woman. His head swiveled as he searched for her. Spotting something shining in the grass, he pushed to his knees and leaned forward to grasp the item. He lifted it, staring in confusion at the black cat face earring.

He stilled as he felt something behind him, a stir in the air that sent a warning through his body. He rose to his feet and spun around, his magic ready to launch at his enemy.

But the petite woman standing before him in a black dress with a full skirt halted his movements.

"Eoghan," she said, a slow smiling pulling at her lips.

He dropped to his knees and bowed his head in deference.

A slim finger lifted his chin so he was staring into her lavender eyes. Her long, black hair was pulled over her left shoulder in a fishtail braid. "We've been searching everywhere for you. I felt powerful magic and came to investigate. I'm delighted to find you. But how did you return?"

He glanced back at the dolmen before returning his gaze to Death. There was something different about her. Almost as if she were . . . diminished.

Her smile was sad as she dropped her hand, her gaze holding his. "I'm dying. Bran is stealing not just my magic, but my life force, as well."

Fury ripped through Eoghan as he got to his feet. How could he have forgotten about Bran? He had to find the other Reapers so they could finish him once and for all.

Erith's hand on his arm stopped not just his body but also his thoughts. He frowned as he looked at Death, waiting to hear what she had to say.

She blew out a soft breath and released him. "I know that what happened in your past made you take a vow of silence. You've been an invaluable warrior for me and the other Reapers. I don't know how much time I have left. I no longer have the energy to keep everything going. I have need of you, Eoghan."

He frowned, not liking her words or her tone. But he waited for her to continue. He owed Erith much, and serving her for eternity was just a small part of it. After his betrayal and death, she'd given him life and a reason to continue.

He nodded, letting her know that he was listening.

"I never pushed you to do more than you were willing," she said. "You were a general in the Light Fae army. You—just like Cael—were born to lead. And that's what I need you to do now."

Eoghan shook his head. There was no way he would push Cael out as leader of the Reapers. Besides, Eoghan had no desire to lead.

"You misunderstand. Cael's position isn't in question." She briefly closed her eyes. "I allowed you and your team to believe you were my only Reapers. Over the years, I've accumulated more betrayed warriors. They work in the shadows as my spies, and to back the seven of you if needed."

Eoghan was so shocked that he took a step back.

"These Reapers need a leader. They are very good at what they do, but they lack the cohesiveness to work as a group. What they need is you," she stated.

It was the first time in years that Eoghan wanted to talk. The words jumbled in his head and swirled in a mass as he tried to figure out how to get them out without speaking.

"Bran is about to win," Death continued in a harsh tone. "I can't stop him from taking my magic. He'll eventually assume my position. And he's going to wipe out all the Reapers. For now, he has no idea about the other group. I've kept them hidden because of this. He believes you're gone. With you leading the others, you have an advantage over Bran that could stop him."

How could Eoghan refuse? But not returning to his brethren would kill him. Cael and the others were his brothers, his family.

As if reading his mind, she said, "Find Cael. Tell him what you're doing."

Eoghan gawked at her. Him? Why wouldn't Death fill Cael in?

Her face fell, a flash of regret quickly passing over her features. "You saved Cael from Bran's magic, but the battle didn't end. Bran turned Neve's brother Dark, and he betrayed and killed her."

Eoghan nodded in understanding. Talin had fallen hard for the Light Fae, and with Neve's betrayal and death, she had taken Eoghan's spot with the Reapers.

"Your brethren have never stopped looking for you. They need to know you've returned." Death gave him a smile. "I knew you would find your way back."

In the next instant, Erith was gone. Eoghan stared at the spot where she had been for several minutes, thinking over all Death had shared—and wondering what she had left out.

He fisted his hand that held the cat earring, the back poking into his palm. There was a deep, profound longing to hear the music that had called him back to Earth. Was it the woman who'd pulled him through the portal that played the music?

He'd only gotten a quick look at her before passing out. Shoulder-length, blue hair, sienna brown eyes, and a tiny diamond stud in her nose. But even with that brief glimpse, he'd recognized her as a Halfling.

A frown formed when he recalled that he'd spoken to her. He'd told her to run. And it appeared as if she had done just that. It was for the best. She was much better off staying far away from him and the war.

Eoghan began walking. It didn't take him long to realize that he was in Ireland. He briefly thought of going to Inchmickery, the small isle off the coast of Scotland near Edinburgh that the Reapers used as a base, but he wasn't ready to be among his brethren just yet.

Instead, he veiled himself and teleported into a copse of trees just outside the Light Castle. And he watched. At one time, it had been a beacon for him, a place that he believed would outshine the Dark Fae in all ways. It didn't matter if it were the castle on Earth or the one on the Fae Realm that was destroyed.

Just because a Fae was Light, didn't mean they couldn't turn Dark. His wife was a prime example. How had he been so blind to the fact that she wanted power? His position had given her just that, but it wasn't enough for her.

The pain of her betrayal no longer cut as deeply after so many thousands of years. It was a dull ache now. But it would never leave him.

Perhaps it was time to put aside his silence. He couldn't lead the Reapers if he didn't talk. Damn. This was going to be harder than he thought.

He was about to teleport away when he spotted Rhi off to his left, hiding in some trees not far from him. The infamous Light Fae who'd fallen in love with a Dragon King was of interest to Death. So much so that Erith had Daire following Rhi.

Yet, as Eoghan sought a glimpse of his friend, there was no sign of Daire. A Reaper could see any Fae—veiled or not. Without a second's thought, Eoghan dropped his veil. Immediately, Rhi's head jerked to him.

"Eoghan," she said as she released her veil and walked to him. She looked him over, a grin forming as she tossed back her long, black hair. "We didn't know what happened to you." Her smile froze when she looked into his eyes.

He frowned, wondering what had caused such a reaction.

"Look, hunky, I'm not a mind reader. I know the human adage of 'silence is golden,' but not in this instance. I need you to talk to me."

Eoghan hesitated. He swallowed twice before he asked, "What's . . . wrong . . . with . . . me?"

"Your eyes. They're silver but . . . different."

He formed a mirror in his hand and looked into it. Rhi was right. His eyes were different. No longer did he have a pupil showing. All he saw was metallic silver staring back at him.

Rhi wrinkled her nose. "You might want to think about using glamour or wearing sunglasses when around humans."

He made the mirror vanish and gave her a nod.

"Are you going to tell me how you got back? Where were you?"

"Tonight. Not sure."

Rhi sighed dramatically. "Well, I guess I should be happy that I'm getting answers at all. Have you seen the others?"

Eoghan shook his head. "Where's Daire?"

She shrugged indifferently, but she couldn't quite hide her pain. "I don't know. One day he was following me, and then he wasn't." Rhi suddenly put her hand on his arm. "I'm glad you're back. Cael and the others have been beside themselves with worry."

He didn't get a chance to reply because she teleported away. Eoghan blew out a breath. It was time he spoke with Cael. He teleported to a cliff on the east side of Ireland and said his old friend's name.

Within moments, Cael was standing before him. Their gazes met. The relief on Cael's face made emotion well up in Eoghan's throat. He'd never had a brother, despite wishing for one. The Reapers were his family, but Cael was like a true brother in every sense of the word.

They embraced before Cael grabbed his shoulders and stepped away to look at him. There was a slight frown when Cael saw his eyes. "Where have you been? How did you get back? When did you get back?"

"One at a time."

Cael's smile vanished as he dropped his arms and stared in shock. "You're speaking?"

"Death said I must."

All emotion was wiped from Cael's face. "She spoke with you?"

"Aye," Eoghan said carefully, wondering what he'd missed out on between Cael and Erith. Because there was definitely tension between them now.

"When?"

"This night."

A muscle ticked in Cael's jaw. "I'm glad she spoke with you since she won't answer any of my calls."

There was much Eoghan had seen that others missed while they stood talking. Because of his vow of silence, Eoghan observed things more closely than others. It's how he knew Cael had feelings for Death—feelings that Cael would never act on. But they were there.

"She's dying," Eoghan said.

Cael ran a hand down his face. "You could see it?"

"Yes."

He turned away and put his hands on his hips as he stared out over the sea. "Why won't she respond to me?"

"I don't think she wants you to see her. I believe if she'd had a choice, she wouldn't have shown herself to me."

"What did she say?" Cael asked as he turned his head to Eoghan.

"Apparently, we aren't the only Reapers. She's asked me to lead another group."

There was no surprise in Cael's eyes as he dropped his arms and faced Eoghan. "I always wondered if she'd stopped finding others like us. I agree with her naming you as their leader."

"Bran doesn't know about them."

"This information will remain between us. Where are they?"

Eoghan shrugged. "I didn't ask, and she didn't say."

Cael shot him a crooked smile. "That sounds like Death."

"How are the others?"

"Good. There is much I need to catch you up on. Fintan fell in love."

Eoghan gaped at him. "You jest."

"Afraid not, old friend. And he isn't the only one. Daire has, as well."

Eoghan listened raptly as Cael retold the stories.

CHAPTER

three

Thea had never driven her car so fast trying to get back to Dublin. She couldn't stop shaking, not even once she was back in her own flat.

All she kept seeing was the man's eyes and the bubble that had formed in his hands. An orb that destroyed the portal stones.

She sat against her headboard with her knees drawn up to her chest, waiting for dawn. Except the sun did nothing to dispel the fright that had taken a firm hold of her. How was she supposed to live now?

A man had come from the dolmen. He'd literally pulled himself out—with her help.

Then he'd instructed her to run.

She hadn't needed to be told twice. Thea had grabbed her violin and ran to her car. It wasn't until she was halfway to Dublin that she wondered who the man was.

Perhaps she should've asked where he'd come from. And just

what had been trying to get through after him. For all she knew, the man was here to harm others.

Thea sighed and dropped her forehead to her knees. She didn't need anything else to be anxious about. But she was a worrier.

She closed her eyes and tried to think of anything but the man. His face was imprinted on her memory, though.

Thick, lustrous, black hair had hung down his back. It had been windblown with strands cutting across his face. His features were strong and defined, noble even. Black brows cut over impossibly thick-lashed, quicksilver eyes. His lips were wide and had been firmed into a harsh line. Then again, he had been fighting for his life.

When he'd landed on top of her, she had felt his strength, the powerful sinew beneath the skin. He could've snapped her neck without breaking a sweat. Instead, he'd protected her.

She couldn't stop seeing his eyes in her mind. It must have been a trick of the light. No one had silver irises like that. And he had to have a pupil. She just hadn't seen it.

Thea lifted her head and scooted off the bed. After a shower and some breakfast, she tried to sleep. When that didn't work, she read the rest of the morning. It was sometime after lunch when she finally managed to dose for a couple of hours. Then, it was time to get ready for the show.

It wasn't until she went to put on her favorite cat earrings that she remembered wearing them the night before. She checked her ear and found only one. Those were her favorite pair.

She took out the remaining stud and chose another set. The Betsy Johnson jewelry was some of her favorites. Tonight, she opted for the crown and scepter mismatched pair.

Thea shrugged into her favorite coat—one she'd designed. A black piece that fell past her knees and laced up the back to conform to her figure. There were also laces along the outer seam of her forearms.

With her violin case in hand, she walked from her flat and out into the street. The tavern where the band performed was only a few blocks away. Most times, she walked it, even in bad weather.

She rarely got sick, but in truth, there was just something about getting out in the air and walking. Many of those around her missed so much by being absorbed in technology or distracted by other people.

Thea loved the architecture of her city. She adored the sights, the sounds, and especially the people. It was those who moved about Dublin that made the city as vibrant and infectious as it was.

When she reached The Deacon, she made her way to the back entrance of the pub. She greeted Duane, who was flirting with a girl. Thea smiled as she walked past him until she found Noah drumming on the walls, the beat of some music playing in his head that only he could hear.

"Hey, Thea," he said with a nod.

She smiled, noting that he'd opted to keep his dark hair in a mohawk with the sides of his head shaved. After she'd turned the corner, she found Josh tuning his guitar with their manager, Annie, beside him.

Josh lifted his blond head and smoothed his hands over the stiff locks fashioned a la David Beckham. "Hey."

"There you are," Annie said as she blew a curl of strawberry blond hair out of her blue eyes. "I thank God every day that Duane found you. All of their testosterone drives me batty. And because you keep me sane."

Thea laughed. "What did they do now?"

"What haven't they done?" Annie cried as she followed Thea. "If you look at them, you'd mistake them for adults, but I swear the fairies got to them because they're children. Silly, irrational kids."

Thea stiffened at the mention of fairies. They were part of Irish legend, and thereby Irish culture, but she'd always gotten a peculiar feeling whenever they were mentioned.

She forced a smile as she set her violin down on a chair and faced Annie as she removed her coat. "Fairies?"

Annie rolled her eyes and sighed. "Sorry. I've been reading some of the Irish folktales to my niece and nephew. You bailed on me last night. What happened?"

"I just wanted some time alone."

Annie flattened her lips and shot Thea a hard look. "You went to the portal stones again."

"I couldn't pass up the opportunity."

"But you forgot me."

Thea's mouth fell open as she realized she had done just that. "Oh, God, Annie. I'm sorry. I'm a horrible friend."

Annie waved away her words. "As soon as you left, I knew that's where you were headed. I got a ride home with Noah."

Thea grinned. "Did he hit on you again?"

"He really doesn't get the hint, does he?" Annie asked in a conspiratorial whisper.

"Maybe because he sees what the rest of us do—that you've got it bad for him."

Annie refused to meet her gaze as she looked for something to do. "You know, I've got . . . there's something I need to see to. Bye."

Thea laughed as Annie hurried away. Annie was the brains behind their band. It was the woman's connections that got them such great gigs and kept them at The Deacon a couple of nights a week.

Annie was organized, ambitious, and one of the nicest people

Thea had ever known. It didn't hurt that Annie could talk anyone into doing whatever she wanted. The fact that they were the only two females in the band had made them gravitate to each other.

It wasn't long before they became fast friends. While Annie was the type always on a call or texting, Thea was just fine losing her phone for days at a time so she didn't have to talk to anyone.

And Annie respected that.

Thea opened her case and took out her violin. She checked the strings and then moved off by herself to warm up. After only a few notes, she felt transported back to the portal stones. With her eyes closed, she saw the dolmen, and the hand reaching out to her.

She kept playing but left her eyes open, hoping the memories would leave her alone. No such luck. This time, she saw liquid silver eyes and heard a hoarse voice telling her to run.

Thea stopped playing and shook her head while attempting to find her focus again. There was a whistle behind her. When she looked, it was Josh, motioning that it was time for them to go on stage. She glanced at the clock on the wall to find that thirty minutes had gone by seemingly in a blink.

She made her way to the raised platform and took her place on the right side. Her gaze scanned the thick crowd, but she didn't see . . . who? Who had she thought to find?

Clearing her throat, she nodded at Duane to let him know she was ready. After a quick introduction, Noah called out a four-count and drummed the first beat. Josh came in with the guitar, and Thea followed an eight-count later. As soon as Duane began to belt out the song, Thea found herself engulfed by the music.

For a moment, she had been really worried that whatever had happened at the dolmen would affect her music as well as her mind, but all was well again.

She smiled as they moved from song to song. After their first set, they took a break where she downed an entire bottle of water in seconds. Then, they were back on stage once more.

Thea loved that they played their own music but also covered popular tunes as well as songs from their heritage. It was a nice mix that kept their popularity growing.

Their second set came to a close, and Thea walked off stage even as men called out to her. She ignored them. She grabbed another bottle of water and lifted it to her lips to drink.

"They're some handsome ones out there tonight," Annie said from beside her.

Thea shrugged and put the cap on the now empty bottle. "I'm not looking for anything."

"But they say that's when you find it."

For some reason, Annie felt it was her mission to find Thea a man. And Thea didn't have the heart to tell her friend to stop. She'd attempted to remind Annie that she was content with the way things were, but Annie didn't listen.

Thea couldn't explain why she didn't want a relationship. She got lonely, incredibly so sometimes, but that didn't change things. Just as she knew she had to go to the portal stones, she knew to remain alone.

"I'll pass," Thea said.

Annie stepped in front of her. "I know you like your space. I know you like going off on your own, but do you ever wonder if you keep people at a distance because you were an orphan."

"I'm still an orphan. That fact will never change."

"I just want you to be happy."

She raised a brow. "Like you? Are you going to take Noah's offer? He's put himself out there for you numerous times. You want him. Take him. How much longer do you think he'll wait?"

Thea walked past her to retrieve her violin for their last set. She shouldn't have been so harsh with Annie, but her friend needed to heed her own advice.

The crowd cheered as the band returned to the stage. Thea put her instrument on her shoulder and raised her bow. She waited for her bandmates to give her a nod, and then she pulled the bow across the strings.

The song was an exciting, hypnotic piece that stirred a special place in her soul. She closed her eyes and let herself be transported to a place far, far away. Somewhere she belonged, somewhere she felt . . . connected.

Heat suddenly rushed over her body. It was heady and exciting. And sensual. She opened her eyes and scanned the crowd. She found him towards the back, standing just on the edge of the dim lighting. His black hair was loose with part of it falling over his thick shoulder.

He had his arms crossed over his chest as he stared. At least she thought he was staring at her. She couldn't tell since he wore sunglasses. But she knew it was him.

Her heart started to pound. He remained in his position for the entire set of songs. And she knew because she couldn't take her eyes off him.

When the last note of the final song played, she lowered her arms but kept her gaze on him. She didn't care that others were calling her name or that she was drenched in sweat. He had come. And she didn't know why.

She backed up a step before turning on her heel and making her way to the rear of the stage. Thea put her violin up before she dabbed a towel on her face to get most of the sweat off. Her hands were shaking when she put on her coat and grabbed her case.

Even as she walked to the back entrance of the tavern, she knew he would be there. Her steps were slow, her heart slamming against her ribs. She had helped him. Surely, that counted for something.

She slowly opened the door and stepped outside. Thea looked around as the heavy metal door slammed behind her. There were shadows everywhere.

"It was you," came the deep, raspy voice.

His Irish accent was thick, his words gruff as if he hadn't spoken in a long time. She turned her head in the direction of the voice.

He stepped from the shadows into the light from above the door, this time without the sunglasses. He was taller than she remembered. He also wore different clothes—clean ones. The dark shirt conformed to his upper body like a glove, showing off his defined physique.

"It was your music that helped me escape."

"Escape?" she repeated.

"Thank you," he said as he came closer.

She couldn't look away. Her gaze was drawn to him like a moth to a flame. His mouthwatering features, his air of dominance. It drew her like a magnet. "Who are you?"

"You saved my life. I'm indebted to you until I can repay what I owe."

No one had ever been beholden to her before, and she had to admit that she quite enjoyed having such a hunk in that position.

CHAPTER

four

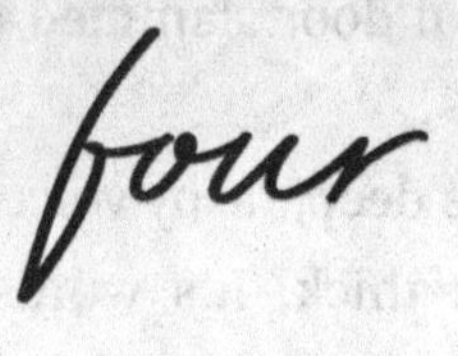

Even over the noise of the city, Eoghan heard the violin. As soon as the first strains of the song reached him, everything else faded away. He couldn't ignore the music any more than he could stop using magic.

He hadn't known what drew him to Dublin—until he heard the strings. The closer he got to the pub, the more the music seemed to wrap around him, tugging him near. And holding tightly.

Eoghan didn't mind. In fact, he sought out the sound. He needed to know who played the instrument. Was it the pretty woman who'd helped pull him through the portal? Or someone else?

Remembering Rhi's words about his eyes, he called forth a pair of sunglasses and put them on before entering the tavern. The place was packed with people as eager as he was to hear more of the music. He shouldered his way through until he found a place near a wall. Normally, this kind of crowd sent him the other direction, but tonight, he didn't think of leaving.

As soon as his gaze landed on the woman swaying as she played the violin, he inwardly smiled. Her blue hair wasn't something he would ever forget. The mix of various shades of blue suited the tempestuous nature he'd glimpsed in her gaze the night before.

She had her eyes closed, completely lost in the music, moving from one song to another without missing a beat—as if she were performing for the notes, not the people. Slow or fast, it didn't matter. The woman had serious skill.

Then again, he expected nothing less from a Halfling.

He eyed her black jeans encasing long legs and the black lace, long-sleeved shirt that scooped low in the front to reveal just a hint of cleavage. The black, high-heeled boots elongated her legs.

There was a flash of sparkle through her hair. Eoghan then spotted the mismatched earrings through the strands. One was a crown that hung from rhinestones, and the other a scepter.

Some might argue that her blue hair and shiny jewelry drew attention, but Eoghan knew the truth. Most only saw her hair or the solid black clothes and looked away in disgust or stared at her tresses, trying to figure out the exact shade. Few ever really noticed her face.

It was the perfect disguise for a half-Fae wanting to blend in.

Compared to her bandmates who were eating up the attention of the crowd, the Halfling was almost removed from it all. As if she preferred solitude but endured people in order to share the music that fell as easily from her as breath.

Eoghan's lungs seized when she suddenly opened her eyes and locked gazes with him. Even from a distance, he knew those orbs held every shade of brown imaginable from a mix of raw umber and caramel to flakes of dark brown.

There was the slightest parting of her lips to let him know she recognized him. Now that he knew she was the one who had led him out of the darkness as well as pulled him through the portal, he owed her a great debt—one he feared might never be repaid.

He intended to cast magic that would alert him if she were ever in danger from humans or the Dark, but especially from Bran. He planned to do it as he followed her home.

When the band played their last song and walked from the stage, Eoghan made his way to the back of the pub to wait. He knew as soon as the door opened that it was the Halfling before she even stepped out.

He hadn't planned to talk to her or even let her know he was near, but then he looked at her face. The next thing he knew, he'd spoken. The words sounded rough and raw, even to his ears.

Her head swiveled to him, and he walked from the shadows straight to her. The soft curve of her lips when he told her that he was in her debt made his blood heat. It took a moment for him to realize that it was lust that burned through him. It had been a long, long time since he'd felt it.

Memories from the night before as he'd covered her body with his when the dolmen exploded filled him. He recalled the softness of her body, the warmth of her skin. The smell of mint from her hair. He wanted so badly to touch her that he fisted his hands.

Death had sent him on a mission. Already, Eoghan wasted valuable time seeking out the Halfling. He needed to cast his magic and leave.

But she was near enough to touch. By the stars, it had been too many eons since he'd last yearned for the touch of another. If only the Halfling would raise her hand to his cheek or even his shoulder. Anything.

So long as she put her hand on him.

"I'm Thea. Thea Keegan," she said. She raised a brow. "And you are?"

He parted his lips to answer when something materialized behind her. The Dark smiled at Eoghan. Without hesitation, Eoghan grabbed her against him and spun, bending over her and acting as a shield so the force of the magic landed on his back.

Blistering pain zapped through him as ball after ball of magic pummeled him. There was no time to fight the Dark, not with Thea. He glanced at her before he teleported both of them away to the roof of a building.

His knees gave out, pitching him forward. Eoghan caught himself with one hand and struggled to keep from falling on top of her.

"You can let go," she said.

His muscles were locked with pain. It took a couple of tries before his arm finally released her. She moved from beneath him and climbed to her feet. Eoghan dropped his head and used both hands to keep from falling on his face.

"Dear God," she murmured from beside him.

He closed his eyes and let his body heal the wounds. The Fae's magic ate away at his skin, muscle, and bone like acid. One of the perks of being a Reaper was faster healing, as well as stronger magic than other Fae, but that didn't make the pain any less excruciating.

The minutes ticked by without another sound from Thea. She remained beside him, and he could only imagine what was going through her head. Though he was immensely grateful that she wasn't bombarding him with questions.

When most of the throbbing diminished to a level where he could breathe easier, Eoghan rocked back onto his haunches and rested his hands on his thighs. Then he opened his eyes and turned his head to her.

Thea's face was a mix of panic, alarm, and curiosity as she set her violin case by her feet. Her brown eyes held his as she squared her shoulders. "I believe you were about to tell me your name."

No hysterics, no demands, no fear. The more he was around Thea, the more he liked what he saw.

"Eoghan."

"It's nice to meet you, Eoghan. I don't suppose after what happened last night and just a moment ago that you'd feel the need to fill me in, would you?"

He rotated his shoulders, stretching out his newly healed skin before he removed the remnants of his shirt. Then he climbed to his feet and used his magic to replace the garment with another.

Thea's eyes briefly widened, but she stood her ground and waited.

"Why do you color your hair so?" he asked.

She hesitated only a minute before replying. "I like to do something different."

"It's not to keep other's eyes off your face?"

Her brows snapped together. "How . . . ? Why would you ask that?"

"Those like you either embrace who they are or hide. The hiding seems to be instinctual, I've found."

"Those like me?" she repeated, her frown deepening. "What's that supposed to mean?"

Eoghan looked out over the city. He really wished Cael or one of the other Reapers were there to tell her. He was never very good at imparting such news.

"Eoghan," she urged.

His gaze swung back to her. "Why do you dye your hair?"

This time, she didn't pause in answering. "Because people look at it and not my face. And before you ask, I don't know why I don't want others to look at me."

"It's because you have Fae blood."

She swallowed nervously and dropped her arms. "I see. Did I bring us up here?"

"I did that." When she stared at him blankly, Eoghan sighed. "You're getting a crash course in this, and I'm sorry about that. I'm a Light Fae. The man who attacked us in the alley is Dark Fae. You can spot them because of their red eyes and the silver in their black hair."

Thea nodded slowly, her face blank.

"I had no intention of telling you any of this. I was going to leave, but the Dark showed up."

She continued to nod, her face folding into anxious lines.

"Are you understanding me?"

"You're Fae. I'm half-Fae."

He lifted one shoulder in a shrug. "Aye. That's the gist of it."

"I need more."

Eoghan ran a hand down his face. What she wanted was for him to talk more. After so many millennia of silence, he was finding it difficult.

"Do you not want to tell me?" she asked.

He shook his head. "Until you pulled me from the portal stones, I went a very long time without speaking."

"Oh." She shoved a lock of hair from her face. "If it's too much, then don't—"

"The Fae come from another realm, but our civil war destroyed vast parts of it. Most have chosen Earth as their home. Ireland, in particular. The Light Queen takes the north, and the Dark take the south."

Thea blinked, her lips forming an O.

"I'm part of an elite team who is hunting a rather nasty Fae bent on slaughtering Death. Aye, Death is a person," he said when he saw the question fill her eyes. "Bran has become a nuisance that has to be stopped. He was the one who sent me to that other realm with a beast that was hunting me. I heard your music and followed it right to the doorway the Halflings and Druids built eons ago to go between realms."

She blew out a long breath. "I think I need a drink."

"It's the mention of the Druids that got you, isn't it?" he teased.

Her look of disbelief faded as she rolled her eyes. "You don't look like someone who jokes."

"I'm not, but you looked like you needed the distraction."

She smiled, laughing softly. "I did. Tell me how you know I'm part Fae?"

"You've the look of us. It's your beauty, but a Fae always recognizes another. Does no one in your family know?"

Thea hunched her shoulders as she shivered against the cold. "I'm an orphan."

"So am I." He wasn't sure why he told her that. It was a part of his past that he rarely thought about. "We should get you out of the night air."

She looked at his outstretched hand. "You brought us here, right?"

"I did. And I'm going to take you wherever you want to go."

"Really?" she asked with a tantalizing grin. "Anywhere?"

He nodded. "Anywhere."

"I want to see the pyramids of Egypt."

Eoghan kept his hand out and waited for her to take it. She

studied him as she reached for her violin case. As soon as her palm slid into his, he teleported them to the great pyramid.

"Bloody hell," she murmured and stumbled back, nearly dropping her case when she spotted the monuments.

He steadied her with a hand as her head tilted back to take in the grand structure before her.

"You really are Fae."

It had been a long time since Eoghan was around anyone with so much enthusiasm. He was supposed to be finding the other Reapers, though Death hadn't told him how to do that. But he couldn't seem to leave the beautiful, beguiling Thea just yet.

Her head turned to him. There was a huge smile on her face as her eyes sparkled with excitement. "I've always wanted to travel. The pyramids have always fascinated me. Thank you for this."

The smile that had begun to form on his face died when he spotted the veiled Fae about two hundred yards away. A quick glance around showed five more.

It looked as if he didn't need to find the Reapers. They had found him.

five

The tightening of Eoghan's face pulled Thea's attention from the magnificent pyramid. His gaze was focused on something over her shoulder.

She let her eyes move around him. The last time he had gotten like that was when they had been attacked. By a Dark Fae.

Thea couldn't believe she was standing with an actual Fae. She wouldn't have believed a word he said if she hadn't pulled him from the portal stones, teleported to a rooftop, watched the atrocious wound on his back heal, and been transported to Egypt in a blink.

But the truth was before her. How could she disregard any of it?

"What is it?" she asked.

Eoghan's quicksilver gaze slid to her. "You're safe."

"You say that like you're about to leave."

His hesitation was answer enough.

She looked up at the cloudless sky with the full moon hanging over them. Lights set up by the government drenched the pyramids and the sand. While she didn't want to get stranded in Egypt, this might be her only chance to see the structures that had interested her since she was a little girl.

"I used to pretend I was an ancient Egyptian," she told him. "My clumsy six-year-old hands did a horrible job mimicking their eye makeup. Years of practice made me an expert. Every Halloween, I dress up as an Egyptian." She glanced at him. "I'm trying to tell you that I'll be fine. Just don't leave me here."

A hurt look flashed across his face. "I would never do such a thing."

"Well, I don't really know you, now do I?"

Eoghan bowed his head. "I won't be far."

"What about the authorities?"

"They won't bother you."

She glanced at the pyramid with a smile. When her gaze returned to Eoghan, he was gone. Thea shrugged and walked closer to the structure. She switched her violin case to her other hand and pressed her palm against the rock.

Residual heat from the sun still warmed the stones. She stood before thousands of years of history. The idea that an ancient Egyptian might have stood where she was sent chills down her spine.

She leaned her head back to look at the very top of the structure. She wanted to climb to the pinnacle and spread her arms wide, taking in the grandeur of the all that the Egyptians had created for others to marvel.

Thea turned and looked at the back of the Sphinx. There were mysteries yet to be discovered beneath the sand, she was sure of it. But she wouldn't be the one to find them. While she craved to know all the Egyptians had created, her calling wasn't to search for that truth.

Though she wasn't sure what her calling was. She knew what she loved, and that was enough.

She slowly turned in a circle, hoping for some sign of Eoghan, but she was the only one there. She felt insignificant next to the massive monuments surrounding her. Some might even feel fearful alone in such a place. But she reveled in it.

Thea moved back several paces from the pyramid. How could she stand in such a place and not play? She lowered her case to the sand and opened it. Then she took out the violin and rested it on her shoulder.

She took a deep breath and pulled the bow over the strings, letting her emotions flow through the music and form in her mind as they moved to her hands before filling the air as song.

It was the most astonishing, breathtaking moment of her life.

There was no running for him. Not that Eoghan would do such a thing. He teleported to the closest Reaper and waited for the others to come to him.

The six stood in a line before him. Three Dark and three Light, five males and one female. As he looked into each of their faces, their names, betrayals, and deaths filled his mind—a gift from Death, no doubt.

Knowing how each of them had lived and what made them stand out to Death allowed Eoghan to know them as she did. As it was, two of them would be handfuls. Not that he could blame them after seeing their stories.

Eoghan's gaze landed on the tallest of the group. Cathal was a giant, his shoulders wide and his red gaze intense. Cathal had left his black and silver hair long with the top portion gathered at the back of his head. He was battle personified. It was in his bearing and even the way he wore his clothes. Unlike most Fae, he kept his sword strapped to his back.

Their gazes clashed, Cathal's lips flattening. Eoghan recognized that despite his rough edges, Cathal would be fiercely loyal.

Eoghan gaze slid to Rordan. The Light Fae had a cocky air about him. Smug with a smartass response always at the ready, Rordan made as many friends as he did enemies. His pain was carefully concealed behind his silver gaze. He kept his black hair short and had an affinity for knives.

Next was Bradach. The Light Fae looked as if he should be behind a desk, but Eoghan knew how looks could be deceiving. The way Bradach's silver gaze continually scanned the area for threats was a dead giveaway.

Beside Bradach was Dubhan. There was a ferocity to the Dark that Dubhan didn't attempt to conceal. His red eyes held no quarter, no forgiveness. With his black and silver chin-length hair, he was every inch a Reaper.

Eoghan moved his eyes to Torin. The Light Fae stood with his arms crossed over his chest, a bored expression on his face, belying the rage that consumed him. It's what made him an incredible warrior, but because he couldn't control his fury, it could put others at risk. With his black hair pulled carelessly in a queue at the base of his neck, he stood at the ready for war.

And last but not least was the lone female of the group. Eoghan looked over the petite Dark Fae. He couldn't tell how long Aisling's black and silver hair was because it was put up in a number of braids to keep it out of her face. Her nails were long and painted blood red before being filed into points. She favored a mix of red and black clothes. Her crimson gaze was as sharp as her nails as she returned his stare.

"How much do you know about me?" he asked them.

Bradach was the one to reply. "Death told us how you were one of the first Reapers and fought against Bran."

"We know you sacrificed yourself for Cael," Cathal replied.

Aisling raised a brow. "Since you're here, I suppose that means you pulled yourself out of whatever place you were sent."

At that moment, the first strings of music filled the air. Eoghan drew in a deep breath, feeling a sense of calm descend over him. To his shock, he watched as each of the six Reapers before him seemed to be soothed by the melody, as well.

"Who is that?" Torin asked.

Dubhan said, "She's a Halfling."

"She's powerful," Rordan replied.

Eoghan turned to look at Thea. "It was her music that drew me out of the hell I was in with a beast I couldn't see closing in on me. She helped me find the portal out. Then, she pulled me through it."

"Damn," Torin murmured.

All Eoghan wanted to do was listen to her play, but the Reapers kept him from doing that. He turned his head to the side to talk to them. "Bran doesn't know about us. While no one aligned with Death can harm Bran or his army, it's still an advantage we can use."

A robin came out of nowhere and flew right at Eoghan. It had been a while since Death had used her birds to send messages, but it was a good sign that she was communicating with him.

He held out his hand as the robin dropped a scroll onto his palm. Eoghan didn't watch the bird fly away. He unrolled the paper and read the list of names before he faced his group.

"More souls to call home," Cathal said in delight.

Bradach cut his eyes to Cathal. "Someone has to continue following Death's orders while the other Reapers are busy with Bran."

Eoghan looked up at his group. He tore the paper into six sections and handed each of them their targets. "Death has already decided their fates. You know what you need to do."

"And what will you be doing?" Aisling asked.

Rordan grinned. "As if we need to ask."

Eoghan ignored Rordan's comment. "I'm going to find us somewhere to call home."

Dubhan was the first to teleport out, followed closely by Torin and Cathal. Bradach was next, and then Rordan. Aisling was last. She held Eoghan's gaze for a moment, then bowed her head and left.

Once more alone, Eoghan dropped his veil and walked to Thea. Her eyes were closed. When she played, she gave herself wholly to the notes. It was as if she became one with them, as if they were the reason for her very existence.

Her bow moved slowly over the strings, drawing out the last of the melody until it faded away. Only then did she open her eyes and lower the instrument to her side.

"Did you write that piece?" he asked.

She shrugged half-heartedly and replaced the violin in the case before shutting it. "I play what comes into my head."

"Your music touches people."

Thea rose, a smile on her lips. "Playing makes me happy. I'm blessed to make money doing something I love."

"I don't think you realize what kind of gift you have. The place I was in . . . your music reached me there."

"What kind of place was it?"

"A horrible one. I'd call it Hell. It was dark. So very dark. I couldn't see anything."

Her brown gaze was troubled as she moved a step closer. "You're free of it now."

"Why were you playing at the dolmen?"

Her lips twisted into a smile. "When I was very little, the children's home I was in visited the megalith. I felt . . . something. I couldn't explain it then, nor can I now. It's almost like it was calling to me. I never heard words, not in my head."

"But your soul did."

She nodded. "Exactly. It didn't matter how many times I went back, I still felt that it wasn't done with me yet."

"Do you still feel its call?" he asked.

"No."

Though he was Fae and thousands of years old, there was still a lot about magic Eoghan didn't know. The idea that the portal stones had brought Thea there so he could be released wasn't farfetched.

"You believe it brought me there for you, don't you?" Thea asked.

Eoghan shrugged. "It could be."

"How long were you in that other place? Years?"

"I don't know," he replied. "Time moves differently in other realms, and then there was magic involved."

She sighed and looked away. "Magic. I can't believe we're talking about it like it's a fact of life."

"Because it is for me."

Her head swiveled back to him. "Are there other Halflings out there?"

"More than you would believe."

"Why do I feel like it's a secret then?"

He watched the wind ruffle her blue locks. Each time he looked, he found a different color in them. Some shades were so pale they could almost be white, while others were navy, and still others a vibrant turquoise.

"As I said, this isn't our realm. The Fae came here and soon learned that the realm was protected by powerful beings—the Dragon Kings."

"I'm sorry," she said with a chuckle. "Did you just say Dragon Kings?"

"They walk among your kind, just as the Fae do," he said.

She blew out a breath. "I can't believe we don't know any of this."

"The Dragon Kings go to great lengths to ensure mortals don't know about them. Most Fae could care less what humans see."

"So these Dragon Kings just let the Fae come here?" she asked.

Eoghan shook his head as he made a sound at the back of his throat. "There was a great war. You see, the Dragon Kings protect the humans. And the Dark feed on them."

"Feed?" she asked with a quirk of a brow.

"They suck the souls from them as they have sex. The mortals only feel pleasure until they die."

Thea's eyes widened in shock. "Are you serious?"

"Mortals are drawn to all Fae. They can't stay away."

"No wonder the Dragon Kings got pissed. And the Light? What do you do?"

Eoghan hesitated because as soon as she asked the question, he had the overwhelming urge to taste her lips.

six

The flagrant desire pouring off him caused Thea's knees to weaken. Since Eoghan had come through the portal, she hadn't stopped thinking about him.

When he showed up at the pub with his attention squarely on her, it had sent thrills shooting through her. And when he spoke to her . . . it caused her heart to skip a beat.

Yet nothing could surpass being the center of his attention. He'd brought her to Egypt! But it wasn't just the pyramids. It was Eoghan himself.

He was mysterious and inscrutable, but she couldn't get enough. She felt completely safe despite the attack earlier. The fact that he had saved her, taking the blasts of magic and the pain, only made her want to know him more.

Less than a foot separated them. Twice, he had wrapped his arms around her, and both times had been to protect her. She wanted his touch for another reason entirely.

While the idea of the Dark feeding off human souls was

disgusting, the thought of finding pleasure in Eoghan's arms made her stomach quiver with anticipation.

"And the Light?" she repeated.

His lips parted while his quicksilver gaze bore into hers. Thea swallowed hard. Her pulse quickened, her heart thumped erratically. She couldn't catch her breath.

The pads of his fingers tenderly touched her jaw, caressing downward until his hand fell away. "Once a mortal mates with a Fae, they are forever ruined. No human can ever satisfy them again."

"And a Halfling?"

His nostrils flared. "None of that applies to you. Your Fae blood prevents it."

She moved a step closer to him. "Really?"

His gaze dropped to her mouth. Thea put her hand over his heart and felt the rapid beat beneath her palm. She jerked her gaze to his face, their eyes clashing.

"I . . . can't," he said and backed away.

Thea let her hand drop to her side. She didn't try to hide her disappointment. She had never made the first move on a guy before, and the one time she did, she'd read his interest wrong. It was humiliating.

"The Fae Wars raged for a long time," Eoghan said and cleared his throat as he faced the pyramid. "Eventually, Usaeil, the Light Queen, joined her army with the Dragon Kings and beat back the Dark. A treaty was signed where the Kings agreed not to wipe out all the Fae if we left."

"But you didn't."

Eoghan's gaze slid to her. "Oh, we left. A few remained behind, but the majority departed. The problem was that we had nowhere to go. Little by little, we returned to this realm. The Kings had their own problems, and as long as no mortals were affected, they left us alone."

"Was that wise?"

"It's something the Kings regret now, but as I said, they have their own troubles. Usaeil decreed that any Light who mingled with humans could only have sex with them once. The problem with that is that many such couplings end with pregnancy."

Thea wrapped her arms around her middle. "The Dark kill humans, while the Light leave offspring."

"Yes."

"I have no information about my parents. The people at the children's home named me. They don't even know the exact date I was born."

Eoghan's brow puckered. "I know how difficult that is."

"What happens now? Do you return me to Dublin, and I never see you again?"

"Yes."

"And if I want to see you?"

"If you're ever in trouble, just say my name. I'll hear you."

Trouble. Which meant that unless she truly needed him, Eoghan would never walk into her life again. Sadness filled her so quickly, it felt as if she were choking on it.

But after everything Eoghan had shown her and told her, how could she be angry with him? She was merely a Halfling who had no clue as to her roots in the Fae or even how strong her connection was.

For all Thea knew, she could have generations of Fae blood running through her. Or her father could've been a Fae. Most likely, it was information she would never gain.

She bent and grasped the handle of her case. "I'm ready."

Eoghan looked from her to the pyramid and back. "We can remain as long as you want."

"You said you were part of an elite group. They're waiting for you, aren't they? And I've been holding you up."

"I wanted to bring you here," he stated.

She forced a smile. "In exchange for helping you last night. I appreciate it, but I'm tired."

"My words have hurt you."

Thea quickly shook her head. The last thing she wanted was to bring up her failed attempt at seducing him. "No. It's fine."

"In our group, it was forbidden to have any sort of relationships outside of our circle."

"Oh." Well, that certainly made her feel a little better. Still, it did nothing to halt her attraction—or what she thought she saw in his eyes.

He held out his hand. Thea glanced at it, hesitating a moment before sliding her palm into his. The contact made her shiver with awareness. With one touch, she was cognizant of his strength. Of the power that ran just beneath his skin—the absolute control he had.

She envied that restraint. While there had never been a reason before tonight, she wished she could learn such a skill. Because despite him making it clear that he wasn't interested, her attraction only seemed to grow.

His long fingers wrapped around her hand. But instead of Egypt and the pyramids disappearing, he simply held her hand. Then he pulled her closer.

Thea studied his face, but Eoghan revealed nothing in his features. It was as if his countenance were made of stone. And his mercurial eyes were impossible to read.

"Do they disturb you?"

She knew he was referring to his eyes. "They're unusual, yes, but beautifully striking. Have they always been like that?"

"They changed after I escaped the other realm."

"Do you see differently?"

He gave a single shake of his head.

She liked being so near to him, as well as having his hand holding hers. And she was in no hurry to return home because, once she did, Eoghan would vanish from her life.

"I don't think I'd mind having your eyes. It'd be better than my plain brown."

His brow furrowed slightly. "Plain? Is that what you think?"

A soft laugh passed her lips. "Yes."

"There is nothing plain about your eyes. They hold a multitude of colors. Fawn, honey, chocolate, russet, as well as hints of bronze and copper. They mix and blend together to make a color as unique and individual as you."

Chills raced over Thea. She would never look at her eyes the same again. "No one has ever talked to me like that before."

"Perhaps you've been with the wrong people."

"Yes, I believe I have," she said breathlessly.

God. If she'd been attracted to him before, after such romantic talk of her eyes, she was ready to throw herself at him.

Eoghan caressed the side of her face. "I'm glad I met you, Thea Keegan."

"Thank you for this." There was much more she wanted to add, but it never made it past her lips.

The next time she blinked, the desert was gone, replaced by the sights and sounds of Dublin. She spotted the pub behind Eoghan. So she was right back where she had started.

"Farewell," Eoghan said as he released her hand and stepped away.

She wanted to call him back, but as she searched her mind for something to say, she found nothing. All she could do was stare open-mouthed as he disappeared.

Thea remained in that exact spot for another minute. Then she took a deep breath and turned around. She gripped her case tighter and began the walk to her flat.

She had no idea how long she had been gone. There were still people walking on the streets, but most had found their beds for the night. Her gaze looked through the gaps in the buildings to the sky and noted that it wasn't as dark. When she searched for the moon, she saw that it had begun to sink into the horizon.

Dawn was fast approaching, and while she hadn't had much sleep in nearly forty-eight hours, she wasn't tired. Being around Eoghan had energized her. Was it because he was Fae? Or was it because of the attraction? She might never figure it out.

And it wasn't as if she would ever get the chance to be around him again. That saddened her much more than she wanted to admit, even to herself.

She felt a buzz in her coat pocket and drew out her mobile phone. There were four calls from Annie, and about a dozen texts that began with a casual You ok? and steadily progressed to If you don't answer me, I'm coming over.

Thea's smile died when she realized she couldn't tell Annie about Eoghan. She couldn't tell anyone about him. Everyone would think she was nuts if she mentioned the Fae or that she'd met Eoghan by pulling him from a dolmen.

The mysterious, handsome Light Fae would be hers alone. She wouldn't share him with anyone. He would be close to her heart, the memories replaying in her head daily.

She put away her mobile and thought of the Fae, Dragon Kings, and Druids. It was interesting to know that such beings walked the Earth, but she wasn't obsessed with learning more about any of them except the Fae.

As a Halfling, she should know that other part of herself. Eoghan had said there were thousands of other half-Fae out there. Maybe she would get lucky and find one.

Thea snorted aloud. What was she going to do? Put an ad out there asking for anyone with Fae blood to contact her? It was laughable. It would never work. Which meant she would never learn more than Eoghan had imparted.

She turned the corner and came to a halt when she spotted a man leaning against a building, one foot propped against the brick.

He drew the toothpick from his mouth and tossed it on the sidewalk as he lowered his foot and straightened. Through the shadows and the light of a nearby streetlamp, she noticed his short, black and silver hair.

"So. You're the one who drew Eoghan out."

His words held a sinister threat. She tried to take a step back, but her feet were frozen in place. He moved into the light and smiled, his red eyes flashing with glee.

"I don't know what you're talking about," she said.

He laughed softly, the sound threatening and ominous. "No use lying to me, Halfling. I saw you with him. I came for you this night. Imagine my surprise when I arrived and found the infamous Reaper with you."

Thea's stomach fell to her feet. He was the Dark Fae who'd attacked earlier, but he hadn't been after Eoghan. She had been his quarry.

"What do you want?" she demanded in a voice that was far stronger than she felt.

He chuckled again. "I want a great many things. You, for one, but I also want you to tell me about Eoghan."

"If you're referring to the man I was with—"

"He's a Reaper," the Dark stated.

She swallowed and lifted her chin. "I don't know what that is. But the man I was with told me his name was Todd."

Thea knew the lie was a long shot, but she had to think of something because she wasn't going to help the Dark in any way.

"Keep your secrets, Halfling. I already have all that I need," he declared and grabbed her arm.

CHAPTER
seven

Leaving Thea was the right thing to do. Why then did Eoghan want to go back? He should've walked her home. He should've at least veiled himself and followed her.

But if he had, he wouldn't have left. He would've stayed and kissed her like he'd been yearning to do. By walking away, he gave himself the chance to fight the desire that rode him ceaselessly.

Eoghan remained in Dublin, however. Finding a place for his Reapers outside of Ireland as Cael had done would be the right thing to do. And yet, he found himself searching the city instead.

Something was keeping him in Dublin, but Eoghan had yet to figure out what it was. With time, he would.

He wouldn't even consider that it was Thea that held him there. Even though Death now allowed the Reapers to have relationships, Eoghan preferred to keep things the way they were. It was easier for everyone involved.

Besides, his brethren had found love with those who were able to help in the fight against Bran. He didn't want to test the waters by getting close to Thea and discovering that he couldn't be with her.

He had to stop thinking about the Halfling. She was a distraction he could ill afford, especially now. He struggled under the weight of leadership. His life and all he had done no longer mattered to him after his betrayal and death.

When Erith came to him with an offer to become a Reaper, Eoghan had almost refused her. What his wife had done had broken him. He'd welcomed the blissful darkness of death that would end the ache of watching his son die.

But Death hadn't given up on him. She didn't promise retribution for what was done. Instead, she'd offered him a way to channel the storm of anger and misery inside him.

The Reapers were just what he needed. He'd forged a strong friendship with all of them, but he and Cael had gotten the closest. When Bran betrayed them, he and Cael had immediately stood together against Bran.

So many times, the two of them stood shoulder-to-shoulder and fought. It felt odd not to be with his brethren now. Eoghan wanted nothing more than to refuse the new rank Death had given him and return to the others. But he couldn't. Neve had taken his place, rounding out the group to seven once more.

There had always been seven Reapers. It wasn't as if Eoghan could tell Talin that the love of his life couldn't be in their group anymore because he wanted his place back.

But his group of Reapers now looked to him as he often had with Cael. Against everything, Cael had stood tall and forged a way for them.

Eoghan now had to remember what it was like to lead. He no longer had thousands of men. Instead, he had the bravest, heartiest Fae warriors to stand with him.

Perhaps it was time to shake off the old mantle and step into his new role with excitement instead of trepidation. Bran was still a target, but while his attention was on Cael and the others, Eoghan's band of Reapers could carry out Death's orders and reap the souls of the Fae.

Until it was time to attack Bran.

Eoghan's search for the perfect base took him all over Dublin. He found exactly what he was looking for in the Old City district. The area dated back to medieval times. There were remnants of Dublin's original city walls as well as cobblestone roads.

The Old City district was popular with tourists because of Dublin Castle, as well as St. Patrick's Cathedral. Along with the old, were boutique shops that brought in the new.

As with many ancient structures, the builders sometimes put in hidden areas below ground. Eoghan found such a place in St. Patrick's Cathedral. It was an area locked away that no one had seen in hundreds of years.

It was exactly what his Reapers needed.

The area wasn't large. It consisted of eight empty rooms, all of which branched off from a circular central chamber. He rid each area of decades of spider webs and dirt with his magic.

In the rotunda, he brought in two sofas and four chairs. This was the place where they would gather and talk. The others could choose what rooms they wanted.

With everything taken care of, he called out to each of his team and gave them the location of their base. Once that was done, he walked the rooms while attempting not to think of Thea.

And failing miserably.

Eoghan had assumed it would take him much longer to scout out a place for his team. He'd hoped for hours with his mind occupied. Instead, he was now free to think of things he shouldn't, to yearn for someone he shouldn't.

He stopped beside a thick pillar that held up the weight of the cathedral above him and dropped his head back. He blew out a harsh breath and tried in vain to put Thea from his mind.

But the hunger within him for her was too overwhelming. It clawed at him, slithering through him like a living, breathing entity. He adjusted his hard cock, but it did no good. He craved her with a fervor that was quickly becoming an obsession.

Eoghan closed his eyes and lowered his head. He spread his fingers as he recalled holding her against him. She had instinctively wrapped her arms around him when he turned her away from the Dark.

And when she had made to kiss him—fek! It had taken everything he had not to give in. She had no idea that if she had tried again, he would've caved.

He finally grew tired of thinking about Thea and teleported to the pub. He needed to see her. The mortals were going about their mornings, making their way to jobs. He hadn't asked Thea where she lived, but he could still find her.

Eoghan closed his eyes and sought out her magic. Usually, with Halflings, their Fae blood was so faint that it took a long while to find it. That wasn't the case with Thea.

His eyes snapped open in surprise when he felt the strength of her magic. He let it wrap around him, sinking into his skin. Then he followed the trail to her flat.

She walked the same path almost every day, so her route was easy to find. It wasn't long before he stood before her building. He walked to the door and used magic to bypass the lock. Then he was inside.

Eoghan briefly hesitated in going to see her. Perhaps it would be better if he veiled himself and popped into her home. No, he knew that wouldn't work. He would wish to talk to her.

That in itself would make Cael laugh. There was nothing any of his brethren had tried over the vast millennia that ever got him to utter even one sound. And now, he wanted to have a conversation with a Halfling.

Yes, his world had certainly changed. Maybe it was being thrown into that other realm and continually chased by that beast that did it. Or maybe it was just time.

He walked up the three flights of stairs to her flat, but once he stood before her door, he found he couldn't raise his hand to knock. So many emotions ran through him, the first of which was a loud voice cautioning him about proceeding.

All he needed to do was think of her blue hair and brown eyes for him to know that there was no other way for him. No matter what he tried, he knew he would return to this exact spot time and again.

How then would he ever be able to bid her farewell? While Bran might not know that he was back, it wouldn't take his nemesis long to figure it out. And then, Bran would likely target Thea because Bran did petty, ridiculous things like that.

Mostly because they hurt the Reapers, and Bran wanted nothing more than for them to feel vast amounts of pain. Especially Eoghan and Cael since they had stood up to Bran when the others wouldn't.

Eoghan was turning away from the door when he heard quick footsteps running up the stairs. He quickly called forth a pair of shades and slipped them on his face before the woman appeared.

He recognized her from the pub. She had some sort of job with Thea's band. The woman shoved her strawberry blond curls from her face and came to a halt when she spotted him.

"Who are you?" she demanded.

"A friend of Thea's," he replied.

A thin brow arched in her forehead. "I'm her best friend, and she's never mentioned you. And trust me when I say, we girls always talk about men like you."

Eoghan wasn't sure if he should take that as a compliment or not. "I'm a new friend."

"Then maybe you can tell me where she is."

"I assumed here."

The woman sighed loudly, her face lined with frustration and anxiety. "I've been calling and texting her since she left the pub last night. Thea likes to be alone, but she always responds to me. Always."

Dread filled Eoghan. He turned and knocked. When there was no answer, he grasped the door to Thea's flat. With a bolt of magic from his hand, he unlocked the entry and strode into the flat.

He took no notice of the surroundings as he and the woman rushed through the two-room apartment, calling her name. But Thea was nowhere to be found.

The woman walked from Thea's bedroom and swallowed heavily. "I think something has happened."

"It had to have been after I left her last night."

"What?" she demanded, her brow furrowing. "You were with her?"

Eoghan nodded once. "For a short while."

"How do I know you're not the one who absconded with her? Maybe you're a serial killer."

He needed to calm her quickly. "Why would I return if I harmed Thea?"

"To throw off the authorities," she replied tartly. "Killers do that."

"That implies that I knew you would come when you did. I had no such knowledge."

That stumped her. She crossed her arms over her chest and shook her head as she briefly closed her eyes. "I know something has happened to her."

"I can find Thea," he heard himself say.

The woman dropped her arms, hope filling her blue eyes. "Really?"

"Yes."

"Oh, thank the Lord," she said and looked up at the ceiling. Then she walked toward him and held out her hand. "I'm Annie Higgins. I manage the band."

Eoghan hesitated in taking her outstretched hand. "A moment ago, you called me a serial killer. And now you trust me?"

"I've not slept all night. I've had more coffee in the last six hours than I drink in two days, and I'm worried sick for my friend."

He took her hand then. "You raised valid concerns."

"And you had good points."

He grinned at her. "You still don't trust me, do you?"

"Not at all," she retorted with a wide smile.

Eoghan liked her immediately. He released her hand. "I would expect nothing less. I'm Eoghan."

"Thea never spoke of you. She would have, you know."

"We met briefly a couple of nights ago. I sought her out last night because I wanted to get to know her better."

Annie tucked her curls behind an ear. "Where did you take her?"

Eoghan didn't want to tell the truth, but if he didn't, then Annie would know he lied—which left him no choice. "Egypt."

She rolled her eyes. "I'm being serious."

"So am I."

Her mouth fell open. "Oh my God. You're serious, aren't you?"

"When we returned, I left her in front of the pub."

Annie grunted and raised a brow as she shot him a hard look. "Why didn't you walk her home?"

"Because if I did, I knew I wouldn't leave."

"Oh," Annie said with a slow smile. "So you like her that way, do you?"

Eoghan pursed his lips, refusing to answer.

Which had Annie giving him a knowing wink.

S he was going to be sick. The abject terror and anxiety mixed with the distress of her kidnapping left Thea shaking. And nauseous.

The Dark had taken her before she knew what he'd been about. Then, it was too late. She stood in the corner of the small cottage with her arms wrapped around herself.

There was a roaring fire in the hearth, and plenty of food in the kitchen, but she didn't touch any of it. What she had done was try to leave. But the door and windows wouldn't budge. She even attempted to break the glass, to no avail.

Thankfully, the Dark hadn't made an appearance since depositing her in the croft. Or, at least, she assumed he was the one who'd brought her.

That left her only one option. She drew in a deep breath and said, "Eoghan."

As the seconds turned into minutes, she grew more concerned.

He'd promised to come if she called. But the lack of his presence was all the answer she needed.

Thea moved to the bed and curled up on her side. Her lack of knowledge when it came to the Fae prevented her from understanding what was going on. What she did know was that the Dark had been searching for her. He'd said as much.

The biggest mystery was why? Before Eoghan, there had been no contact between her and the Fae—that she knew of anyway. She kept mostly to herself, but there was a chance she had passed a Fae on the street. Other than that, she couldn't think of any reason the Fae, especially the Dark, would want her for anything.

Unless they knew she was a Halfling.

She rolled onto her back and looked at the ceiling. Was it mere coincidence that Eoghan told her about her Fae blood and then a Dark took her? She didn't think Eoghan would've taken the injury from their encounter with the Dark if the two were working together.

There was a small section of her mind which cautioned that Eoghan and the Dark could have set everything up. Then she remembered pulling Eoghan from the portal stones and the way he had gripped her as if he were dying, as if he were escaping Hell.

As if he wanted to live.

No, she didn't believe Eoghan was working with the Dark. And since the Fae hadn't shown his face since dropping her at the cottage, it looked as though she would have to wait to find out why she had been taken and who wanted her.

"Eoghan," she said again, hoping that he heard her this time.

Once her stomach settled, she rose and walked the inside perimeter of the cottage. It was small but had everything she needed. She even found a closet with clothes in her exact size.

"So bizarre," she murmured and closed the door.

Who kidnapped someone and gave them clothes? Something wasn't adding up, and she didn't like the anticipation of learning the truth.

"Hello!" she called out. "Anyone there? Hey! The Dark who took me! You around? I've got some questions."

She sighed loudly when there was no reply. Not that she'd actually thought she would get one. Not one willing to give up so easily, she went back to the door and tried to open it again. She yanked on the handle, shoved her shoulder against it, and even pounded on the wood, but it didn't so much as creak.

Thea was becoming frantic. She put her hands in her hair and dropped to her knees in the middle of the cottage. Squeezing her eyes shut, she fought to remain calm, but it stayed just out of reach.

She dropped her hands to her sides and opened her eyes. A smile pulled at her lips when she spotted her violin case beside the sofa. She quickly crawled to it and rested the container on its side before opening it.

Thea softly slid her fingers over the polished wood of the instrument. If there was one thing that could bring her peace and help her get control of things to face whatever was coming, it was playing.

She lifted the violin to her shoulder and rested her chin in the groove. Her fingers found the neck as her other hand gripped the bow. After a deep breath, she put the bow to the strings and began to play.

The music instantly soothed her, relaxing her tense muscles and easing her cramped stomach. She lost track of time, which allowed her to forget where she was—and why. It was in the notes that drifted through her that she was able to escape, if only mentally.

She wasn't sure when she became aware of someone in the cottage with her. One moment she was alone, and the next, she wasn't. Thea kept her eyes locked on the floor while using her peripheral vision to try and see something. Anything.

Finally, she lowered the violin and turned to look behind her. But there was nothing. Nothing she could see anyway. Someone had been there, though. She'd stake her life on it. Her gaze moved slowly around the cottage. While her sight picked up nothing, her other senses screamed in warning.

"What do you want with me?" Thea asked. When there was no response, she climbed to her feet. "You have no right to hold me here. I demand to be released."

Not that she expected any kind of response, but it still irked her when nothing happened. Anger started to burn where fear once nestled, like a cold pit in her stomach. She was going to find who was responsible for holding her, and Thea would make them pay.

"Did you hear that?" Eoghan asked Annie.

She raised her brows and gave him a strange look. "You mean the cars outside? The honking horns, and the people talking?"

"I heard music." Matter of fact, he was sure it had been Thea.

"Well, yeah," Annie said with a chuckle. "People play their music loud sometimes."

"No, I heard Thea."

Annie's face lost the sarcasm as she took a step closer. "Do you still hear her?"

He gave a shake of his head. "No."

"You must have really good hearing if you could detect anything over the noise of the city."

Eoghan met the mortal's probing, blue gaze. "I'm attuned to Thea's music."

"If you heard her, then she's not far, right?" Annie asked hopefully.

He strode to the window and looked out. "I've no clue where she is."

"I'm going to call her again."

Annie then took out her mobile and punched a number before bringing it to her ear. Eoghan glanced at her as she tapped her toe impatiently.

After a few seconds, she lowered the phone. "Voicemail."

"She'll play again," Eoghan declared. "I'll find her when she does."

"I want to go with you."

He turned to Annie. "There may not be time for that."

"She's my best friend."

"I will bring her back to you."

Annie put her purse on her shoulder and gave him a sad smile. "You know, for some inexplicable reason, I believe you."

"Good."

"How do I get ahold of you?"

He hesitated, unsure what to tell her. Finally, he said, "Just say my name."

She gave a loud, disbelieving snort. "You can't be serious."

"I am."

"Is this your way of making sure you don't have to talk to me?"

He walked to her. "I've no device that you can call. But I will hear you say my name."

"Your hearing, huh?" She studied him a moment. "Take off your sunglasses."

Eoghan inhaled deeply. He briefly thought of using glamour to hide his eyes before he removed the shades but decided against it. Her face went slack when she met his gaze.

"Who are you?" Annie demanded.

"Someone who can find Thea."

She glanced away, but her gaze was drawn back to his face. "You're asking me to take a lot on faith."

"I never break my word."

"That may mean a lot for those who know you, but I just met you."

He knew she was right. "Even if I had a mobile, I could give you the wrong number or never answer."

"The authorities would have a way to track you."

"Is the band performing tonight?"

She frowned but shook her head. "They have the next two nights off. Why?"

"Go home. Stay there if you can. Don't talk to anyone you don't know. If anything seems out of the ordinary or you hear from Thea, call for me."

"No," she said.

Eoghan wasn't going to spend the rest of the day in a battle of wits with the mortal. He needed to find Thea, and he needed to do it sooner rather than later. He veiled himself as Annie took a breath.

Her mouth fell open as she turned in a circle, looking for him. "What the bloody hell," she murmured. After a few minutes of silence, Annie stalked from the flat, slamming the door behind her as she mumbled obscenities about him.

Eoghan teleported to the roof and listened for any signs of Thea, but there was none of her powerful, magical notes that filled the air and transcended time and space.

He stood there for another hour before he returned to the base below the cathedral. When he arrived, Cathal sat in one of the chairs, his long legs stretched out before him with his ankles crossed.

"How long have you been here?" Eoghan asked.

He shrugged. "A while. My assignment was an easy one."

"And the others?"

Cathal shot him a perturbed look. "I don't know."

"They're your brethren. You should know," Eoghan said.

"We're still working on the group thing."

Eoghan held his gaze. "Work harder. If we don't trust each other implicitly, then we're doomed before we even begin."

Cathal leaned forward and uncrossed his ankles. "Are you angry to have left your group? Or are you excited to be leading now?"

"You know as well as I that we choose who knows our pasts," Eoghan replied. "But you ask a valid question. Before I was a Reaper, I was a general in the Fae army. I was happy to have Cael lead the Reapers. He's a natural at it."

"Some might say you are, as well," Cathal said.

Eoghan shoved his long hair out of his face. "I miss my brothers, but we each have our own paths. Mine deviated from the others' and brought me to you."

"Do you think our group could be as close as your Reapers?"

"You and the others are my Reapers now," he corrected. "But, yes, I believe we could be. We seven are a unit. We will work in conjunction with Cael's team when needed, but we have to be a family. And that means forming bonds of trust."

"Perhaps it should start with you," Aisling said from behind him.

Eoghan turned to find the other five Reapers. He raised a brow. "Meaning?"

"Who are you looking for?" Aisling asked.

He frowned as he took a step toward her. "You followed me?"

"No," she said with a shake of her head. "I saw you when I was on my way here. You looked . . . agitated. That's when I followed you."

The leather in the chair creaked as Cathal rose behind him. "We can help you find whoever it is."

Eoghan looked at the ground as he weighed his options. Finally, he raised his head and shifted so he could see all of them. "The woman who led me to the portal door to return to this realm has been taken."

"You mean the woman from last night?" Bradach asked.

Eoghan nodded slowly. "Thea was taken after I returned her to the city."

"Then let's find her," Rordan stated.

nine

nactivity drove Xaneth nuts. He was an expert hunter. Give him a target, and he could locate it. The more difficult, the better. Which was how he'd gotten the job of finding the Halfling.

Discovering that Thea knew Eoghan was a boon that would net Xaneth a multitude of praise and whatever else he asked for. After living on the outskirts of the Fae his entire life, he intended to use this new information to his benefit.

He dropped the glamour and ran his hands through his black hair. Gathering the length at the base of his neck, he tied it off with a strip of leather and leaned back against the cottage.

Thea alternated between shouting and pounding at the door. He'd much prefer it if she would go back to playing her violin while he waited.

"Xaneth."

He jerked to attention at the voice. His gaze briefly met

swirling silver eyes before he dropped to one knee, bowing his head. "My queen."

"Rise," Usaeil said.

He straightened and looked into the face of ethereal beauty. "I wondered if you'd received my message."

"I rule thousands. My duties never end."

Xaneth clasped his hands behind his back. He didn't bother to tell Usaeil that while he walked among the Dark, he'd heard disturbing tales about her. Those tales, added with what he knew of her actions she kept secret were just some things his ability to move between the Light and Dark gave him.

And if everything went according to plan, she was his ticket back into the ranks of the Light.

Usaeil turned her head to look through a window of the cottage. "She's not ready to speak with me."

"Nor will she be if you keep her locked away."

The queen's gaze snapped to him before narrowing. "You think to tell me what to do?"

"I merely caution you about which actions you might take." Xaneth was nothing if not diplomatic when the need arose. After negotiating dozens of truces with other races, and maneuvering through the landmine that was the Fae, it had become an invaluable asset.

"Caution?" Usaeil asked. "Is that what you're doing?"

Xaneth bowed his head. The Dark Fae now had a new king. The Light were in a tither about Usaeil banishing Rhi. And more shocking, was the new—or old—adversary who went by the name of Bran, who recruited and took Dark for his army.

Xaneth had learned of Bran and the Reapers—specifically, those named Eoghan and Cael—by eavesdropping. Apparently, Bran wanted those two more than anything.

But Xaneth had survived as long as he had because he was vigilant and careful. His position with Usaeil was precarious, and he didn't want to do anything to muddy the waters. Not when Usaeil had the power to give him everything he wanted and more.

"We both know your repentant act is just that. An act," Usaeil said, her eyes narrowing dangerously.

Xaneth met her gaze. He, more than anyone, knew what the queen was capable of. Though he no longer had anything to lose. "You found me because of my reputation. I'm able to hunt anything and run it to ground. I agreed to help because of who you are. And because you can give me what I seek."

Her lips curved into a knowing smile. "I can give you anything you want."

There was something in her tone that gave him pause. A lifetime of running to stay ahead of the Trackers after him had sent up warning signals. But he would never know the outcome if he didn't try. Xaneth just hoped it wasn't a mistake.

"I've retrieved that which you sought. Handing her over to you now shall conclude our business."

"Does it?"

For fek's sake. So this was how it was going to go? He should've known. Usaeil was an enemy—she just didn't realize it. Yet. He had a particular code, and it didn't matter who he dealt with, he never allowed a betrayal to go unanswered.

And to think, he'd decided not to retaliate after what she'd done to his family. Now, he wished he hadn't agreed to work with her.

Usaeil laughed and tossed back her long, black hair. "You look concerned. Why is that?"

"I'm not worried, my queen."

She drew close and peered up into his face, wearing a smile

that was anything but pure. "It's been several millennia, but did you think I'd forget you? Did you really believe that with one act, I would allow you back into the Light? Banishment is forever . . . nephew."

His hands itched to call forth his blades, but he kept control of the volatile rage that bubbled inside him like lava.

"Oh, yes," she stated as she looked at him with disgust. "Frankly, I'm surprised you're still alive. I thought I had all of you hunted down and killed."

He was careful to keep the fury from his face. All the years of watching his family being picked off one by one by the Trackers had left him hollow and bitter. He'd turned those emotions to his benefit—and he'd thought to use Usaeil to his advantage. What a fekking waste.

Now, he was on her radar. No doubt, the Trackers would be after him. But they wouldn't find him easily.

Usaeil's smile was wide as she squeezed her shoulders together. "Your expression is priceless. It's made my day."

He was going to kill her. Or at least attempt to end her life. No one was strong enough to go up against Usaeil except for Balladyn, the new King of the Dark. Or perhaps Rhi. But Xaneth would rather die trying to avenge his family than wait for Uaseil to strike.

"For pity's sake," she said with a roll of her eyes. "Cheer up. I'm not going to kill you. Yet," she added with a raise of her brow.

Yeah. He was definitely going to kill her.

"I tell you what," Usaeil said as she put a finger against her mouth and pursed her lips for a heartbeat. "You stay here as a guard and look over my new . . . acquisition . . . and I'll allow you to live."

She needed him for the moment, which was the only reason he

was still alive. His body vibrated with the need to plunge a blade into her black heart.

Usaeil raised her brows and widened her eyes. "This is the part where you vow to serve me."

Xaneth couldn't form the words. They lodged in his throat, choking him. All his years of forming alliances had gotten him exactly nowhere. His aunt had told him that Usaeil wouldn't stop until every last one of them was dead. He should've listened to her.

"Is this your way of telling me no?" Usaeil demanded. She held up a hand, ready to snap her fingers.

He didn't have to ask to know that she would call one of the Trackers. Usaeil would never dirty her hands by killing him herself.

But he needed time. No betrayal—no matter how small or large—was ever forgotten. Or left unpaid.

Whatever idiocy had made him think that he could prove to her that he wasn't a threat and make her forget her need to kill him flew out the window.

Now, he had another mission. If he couldn't take her out, then he would find someone who could help him.

"I vow to serve you," Xaneth said.

Usaeil pointed at the ground. "Say it on your knees."

He clenched his teeth together. Every fiber of his being screamed for him to attack her. It was only his mind, urging reason, that held him back—that and the image of his sister begging for her life before being struck down by one of the Hunters.

He lowered himself to one knee at a time. His body shook with his fury, as a silent promise ran through him. "I vow to serve you."

She patted his head. "Good boy. Don't do anything stupid. I'll be watching you."

He remained on his knees several minutes after she was gone. His wrath simmered until it boiled over. He threw back his head and bellowed his rage.

Xaneth fell forward onto his hands and squeezed his eyes closed. The image of his sister filled his head. She had been so young, only a child when she was killed. He had left her for only a short time to find them food. When he returned, he'd arrived in time to see the Tracker ignore her cries of mercy and plunge his blade into her chest.

Xaneth had gathered her in his arms after the Tracker left. She opened her eyes long enough to smile before she was gone. Leaving him all alone. Even after thirteen hundred years, he could still feel her body grow cold in his arms.

The fires of his anger engulfed him until he was nothing but flames. And the only thing that would douse them was Usaeil's death.

The pounding on the door drew his attention. He opened his eyes and got to his feet to face the cottage. The one thing he didn't know was why the Light Queen wanted the Halfling. But that could be remedied quickly enough.

Xaneth walked to the door. He didn't touch it or open it. "Nothing is going to harm you," he told the Halfling.

"Let me out," she demanded.

He looked at his hands and thought about his blades. Immediately, both short swords materialized in his palms. "Not yet."

"Tell me why I've been taken."

"I don't know."

There was a slight pause. "But you kidnapped me."

"So I did."

There was a bang as if she had kicked the door. "Then why did you do it?"

He tightened his grip on the hilts of the weapons. "Be calm, Halfling. I'm protecting you."

"Oh, that makes me feel sooo much better," she replied acerbically.

Xaneth grinned despite himself, but it faded quickly. "I'm going to make it so the one who wants you can't get to you."

"Uh . . . thanks?"

"Remain calm."

"How about I lock you away and tell you to remain calm?"

He sheathed his weapons at his back and put his hands on either side of the doorway, the wards spreading from his palms wrapping around the house.

"You're far better with me than the other."

"Tell me who the other is and let me decided that. Better yet, let me go," she said with a heavy dose of sass in her voice.

"Nice try," he told her and stepped away once the cottage had been warded.

It wouldn't keep Usaeil out completely, but it would take her considerable energy to get through them. That would give him enough time to return if she came for the Halfling while he was gone.

Xaneth then used glamour make himself look like a Dark once more before teleporting to the Dark Palace. He walked the halls, listening for anything that could give him information on Bran.

This new adversary that the Light knew nothing about could be the one to take out Usaeil. And with the information he had on Eoghan, it would certainly get him an audience with Bran.

Xaneth knew how lucky he was to have overheard Eoghan give

his name to the Halfling in the alley. If he would've gotten there a moment later, he wouldn't hold such crucial information that could right the wrongs done to his family—intel that had the potential to knock Usaeil's scrawny ass off her throne.

He turned a corner and came up short when he found Balladyn leaning a shoulder against the wall as if he'd been waiting for Xaneth.

The King of the Dark raised a brow. "I have a distinct dislike for a Light who uses glamour in my palace."

Xaneth noted that Balladyn didn't have any guards around. Not that Xaneth was foolish enough to take on the king. Xaneth filed away the fact that Balladyn could see through the glamour for later. "I couldn't exactly come in here without it."

"And why are you here? To try and kill me?" The king straightened and spread his legs as he stared at Xaneth.

"I'm not an assassin, but if I were, you wouldn't see me."

Balladyn briefly narrowed his gaze. "Why are you here?"

"I'm looking for someone who can take me to Bran."

"Bran?" Balladyn repeated, his interest caught. "Why?"

Xaneth frowned. "So, you know him."

"I know of him," Balladyn replied. "I know he's taking Dark against their will. I know he has acquired some powerful enemies."

And Xaneth knew those enemies were the Reapers. "I have information he wants."

The king issued a snort of laughter. "And what do you want in exchange."

"Usaeil's death."

"Well, now," Balladyn said with a grin. "A Fae after my own heart. Why not ask me to do it?"

Xaneth didn't want to take the time to talk his way out of

landing in the dungeon, but he had no choice. "Because the information I have would mean nothing to you."

"Yet it does to Bran?"

"Yes."

"Interesting," Balladyn said as he walked closer. "Especially since I have need of a spy within Bran's ranks."

The news shocked Xaneth. He usually expected things like this, but the king had caught him off guard. "You fear Bran might try and take your position?"

"He's taking my people. I don't like that."

"Why me?" Xaneth asked. "Why would you trust me to spy for you?"

Balladyn grinned. "We want the same thing—Usaeil gone. What do you say?"

Xaneth clasped the king's outstretched hand, realizing that Balladyn could be a good ally. "I say you can never have too many friends."

CHAPTER

ten

Each minute felt like an eternity. Thea returned to the door again and again in the hopes that it might suddenly unlock. And every time, her anger, helplessness, and irritation mounted.

She tried to get the Fae to respond to her again, but once more, he'd returned to silence. Thea had a knack for recognizing voices, and she knew that he was the same Dark who'd kidnapped her and attacked Eoghan.

Just like Eoghan, she assumed the Dark had been after him. It never entered her mind that the Fae would want her. After all, until Eoghan, she hadn't even known she was a Halfling. Now, it seemed as if everyone knew.

Her stomach rumbled, but she refused to eat anything. For all she knew, it was laced with . . . well, she was sure it had something on it, in it, or whatever to make her do things she wouldn't normally do.

"I'm paranoid," she murmured.

Thea immediately walked to her violin and began playing. She had to find some measure of calm. Otherwise, her brain might explode from all the different scenarios that kept running through her head.

She didn't bother calling for Eoghan again. Either he couldn't hear her—or he never planned to respond. She hadn't thought him the type not to answer, but how well did she really know him?

Her eyes squeezed shut when her air of melancholy came through in the notes she played. She had thought—hoped—Eoghan was. . . .

She couldn't finish the thought. Apparently, her attraction to him—the overwhelming, blinding desire—had prevented her from seeing the obvious.

Thea poured her emotions into the music. The melody turned frantic as her worry grew. And with only a thought of Eoghan, the song shifted once more. It became evocative. Haunting.

Somehow, the music was able to say what she could never put into words. And she didn't stop it.

Eoghan's head jerked to the left. He closed his eyes, reaching for the soft melody that drifted on the wind.

His Reapers were behind him. They stood atop the cathedral so he could listen for Thea. He'd known she would play. It was just a matter of waiting and listening for her.

The music teased him, giving him only a few notes at a time. But he would recognize the playing anywhere. Thea's music had a distinct sound to it. One that he would hear even if he were deaf.

His eyes opened as he stared off to the west. "I hear her."

"Go," Torin said. "We'll follow."

Eoghan didn't need to be told twice. He teleported a ways and stopped to listen. The music was louder but still some distance off.

He teleported three more times before he knew he was close. Each time, the Reapers were right on his heels. As he turned to them, he saw the way they looked around, searching for Thea.

"I can hear her now," Bradach stated.

Eoghan slowly turned in a circle to try and locate Thea. "It's because she's close."

Dubhan asked, "Can she veil herself?"

"No," Eoghan replied. "Someone is doing it for her."

"But we should be able to see her," Cathal pointed out.

Eoghan's lips flattened. "Yes, we should."

"Is it Bran?" Rordan asked.

Eoghan shook his head. "If it were, Bran would show himself. He likes to take all the credit. There's no way he could remain hidden instead of showing off."

"Just like a guy," Aisling said with a roll of her eyes.

Eoghan held up his hands and pushed outward, searching for Fae magic. It didn't take him long to encounter a force that made him take a step back.

"Shite," he mumbled.

"What the fek was that?" Torin asked in disbelief.

Rordan shrugged and said sarcastically, "I'm thinking magic."

Torin glared at Rordan in displeasure. Eoghan was ready to stop them when Torin took a step toward Rordan. At the last second, the Light regained his composure and halted. Torin then looked at Eoghan and gave a nod of his head.

Eoghan swung his gaze to Rordan and raised a brow.

The Fae lifted his hands before him and shrugged. "I'm sorry. My mouth opens, and things just spill out."

"Doesn't bother me," Cathal said.

Dubhan turned his head to Torin, who stood beside him. "You need to lighten up, man. Otherwise, you're going to want to beat the shite out of Rordan every other minute."

Aisling looked heavenward as she let out a loud sigh. "Why couldn't there be more females? I have this need to turn around and smack all of you upside the head."

Rordan grinned. "I like being whipped."

Eoghan found their interaction interesting, especially when he noted that all of them were doing their best to get along.

It was Bradach who said, "How do we remove the veil hiding Thea?"

"Fan out," Eoghan told them. "Remain veiled and see what you can find." He looked pointedly at Torin and Cathal when he said, "Do not engage. This is strictly scouting. For now."

One by one, the Reapers teleported away. Eoghan remained and turned in the direction of the music. Thea was close. Very close.

He dropped his veil in the hopes that whoever was keeping Thea from him would reveal themselves.

Xaneth still mulled over his new alliance with Balladyn when he returned to the cottage to check on Thea. He smiled when he saw Eoghan.

He wasn't surprised that the Reaper had found Thea. In fact, he'd expected it. But Xaneth had also expected that Thea would be in Usaeil's hands by now, and the queen would have to deal with the Reaper.

But all of that had quickly gone south. Usaeil's betrayal had made him reevaluate his strategy—and intentions. With Balladyn's cooperation, Xaneth would soon meet Bran. Once he shared the news about Eoghan, Bran would be after the Reaper. But not before taking out Usaeil.

It was the perfect plan. With Usaeil gone, Xaneth could return to the Light—where he belonged. The wrongs done to his family would finally be righted.

He studied Eoghan, who walked toward the veiled cottage. Xaneth frowned. His wards should have ensured that Thea's playing couldn't be heard outside the house. Xaneth could hear her because he'd put the spells in place.

But Eoghan had his head tilted to the side as if he were listening to something. It was only a matter of time before the Reaper found the cottage.

"Show yourself," Eoghan demanded.

Xaneth might be a bit reckless at times, but he wasn't stupid. He had no intention of going up against a Reaper. The only reason he'd taken a shot at Eoghan at the pub was because Xaneth had thought he could get to Thea. But the Reaper had been too quick.

While the majority of the Fae believed the Reapers were nothing but myths, Xaneth knew the truth. He also knew the extent of a Reaper's power.

"I will free her," Eoghan announced.

Xaneth looked at the cottage. No doubt the Reaper could do exactly as he claimed. Usaeil had threatened Xaneth with death, but if his plan worked, the queen would be dead. Why not ruffle her feathers while he could?

The idea was too good to pass up. Xaneth lowered the veil. Eoghan would have to get through the wards himself. He wouldn't make it too easy for the Reaper.

Xaneth really wished he'd be there to see Usaeil's face when she arrived, and Thea was gone. But just knowing the queen would most likely lose her shit in an epic meltdown was enough.

It was his first step in retaliation for her betrayal.

He looked at Eoghan before teleporting away.

"Thea!"

She halted her playing at the sound of Eoghan's voice. With her heart hammering in her chest, she waited for him to speak again so she could confirm that her mind wasn't playing tricks on her.

"Thea!"

She put her violin down and rushed to the door. "Eoghan! I'm here."

"Stand back," he told her. "There are wards around the house that I need to get through."

She took several steps back before turning to rush to the sofa and put away her violin. Her hands shook with excitement. Maybe Eoghan had heard her, but it had taken him a while to reach her. Not that it was relevant now. He was there. That's all that mattered.

There was a loud thwack against the door that made the cottage shudder. A moment later, there was a harder hit. She lost count of how many times something banged as she impatiently waited to be released.

A moment later, there was a loud boom as the door burst open. Thea lifted her arm to shield her face as she turned away. She glimpsed shards of wood coming right at her. Everything moved in slow motion—including her.

Suddenly, strong arms wrapped around her as her ears rang

with the crash. She remained bent over, even as silence descended around her.

"I've got you," Eoghan whispered.

She was so happy to see him that her throat locked with emotion. Thea turned to him and wrapped her arms around his neck. Her fingers brushed wood. She jerked back when she realized that he had pieces of the door sticking out of his back.

"Better me than you," he said.

She looked into his mercurial eyes and put a hand on his face. "Thank you for coming. Let me get the splinters out."

"You'd better let us do that," a man said as he strode into the cottage.

Thea stared in shock as five men—one a damn giant—and a woman filled the cottage. She knew without asking that they were part of Eoghan's group that he'd told her about.

"It's all right," Eoghan said.

Her eyes slid back to him as two men moved on either side of him and a third began pulling out the splinters, some of them as thick as her fist and nearly a foot in length. She knew it had to hurt, but Eoghan never let it show.

"I didn't think you heard my call," she said.

He gave a shake of his head. "I didn't."

"Then how did you find me?"

"Your music," he replied with a small grin.

It had reached him in another realm. This time, her music saved her.

"Do you know who took me?" she asked.

Eoghan's face tightened. "Not yet, but I will."

"Did you not see anyone?" the woman asked.

Thea glanced at the Fae's thick, black and silver hair in

multiple braids. Then her gaze locked with the woman's red eyes. "It was a Dark Fae."

"A Dark?" Eoghan repeated, a deep frown marring his brow.

"The same one who attacked us outside the pub."

"I thought he was after me."

She wrinkled her nose as she shrugged. "It was me. Apparently, someone sent him to track me down."

"Track you down?" one of the men asked, a Light Fae with short black hair and several knives on his person.

Eoghan glanced at the man before returning his attention to Thea. "Did he say what he wanted with you?"

She swallowed and twisted her lips. "I think he was only sent to find me. There was another presence with me for a moment. I felt them but never saw them. That's who I think wants me."

Eoghan straightened as the last of the splinters were pulled from his back. He wrapped an arm around her as he looked at the others. "Search the area. There are clues out there. Find them and bring them to me."

In the next breath, Thea was teleported away.

CHAPTER eleven

Even the most stalwart of men had a breaking point. And holding Thea once more in his arms was Eoghan's. Like the proverbial straw.

He brought her to the base beneath the church. Yet, once there, he couldn't release her. She looked up at him with those gorgeous brown eyes of hers, and he was lost, adrift—and sinking fast—in all that was Thea.

"Where are we?" she whispered.

He swallowed and valiantly tried to make his arms drop away, but his body had other ideas. It had been eons since he'd held a woman in his arms, much less felt desire.

"Eoghan?" she asked with a slight tilt of her head.

"You're safe," he managed to say.

His blood pounded in his ears, and his heart thudded in his chest. All he wanted was a taste of her. Just one small sip of her lips.

Her lids slowly lowered as she blinked. "I know."

The need to kiss her was so overwhelming, so irresistible, that it was all he could think about. His gaze dropped to her lips. They were a temptation all their own. Dark pink with a perfect Cupid's bow, her mouth could bring a man to his knees without a word.

Her top lip was slightly thinner than the bottom, but the minor imperfection was endearing. And sexy as hell. Her mouth promised passion of unequaled delight.

Who was he to turn away from such temptation?

He sought memories long buried as he tried to remember how to proceed to the next step. All the thousands of centuries he'd wrapped himself in the betrayal that changed his world, forgetting the simple pleasures in life.

Eoghan allowed himself to be shut off from everything—except his duty. His fellow Reapers had never pushed him for more, but he hadn't allowed them to get close either. Only Cael.

He didn't remember how to kiss, or even what to do. Surely, it would come back to him. He lowered his head, but as her lips drew near, he hesitated.

Thea then reached up and put her hands on either side of his head as she rose up onto her tiptoes and pressed her lips against his.

All the hunger and longing that had been burning through him since encountering Thea exploded into a frenzy of desire that consumed him.

From the moment their mouths met, Eoghan knew there was no turning back. He tilted his head to the side and moved his lips against hers. They were soft and sweet, her taste like a drug that quickly and effortlessly took him.

A moan rumbled through him when their tongues tangled together in a sensual, carnal dance that had his cock hardening with anticipation.

Her fingers sank into his hair as their kiss deepened. He backed her to a wall and pressed his body against hers. She groaned and scraped her nails lightly on his scalp.

He wanted inside her, to meld their bodies together in a ritual as old as time. His hands trembled as he grasped her hips and ground into her softness.

"Yes," she murmured between kisses.

Eoghan moved his hand upward to the hem of her sweater and slipped beneath. His palm met skin as he caressed the indent of her waist. He reeled from the unadulterated, vibrant desire that swirled around and through him.

Dimly, he recalled that the others would return soon. He knew he should stop the insanity, but he couldn't. Yet he didn't want the others to see them either.

Gathering all of his strength, Eoghan ended the kiss and took several steps back. Thea tipped forward before righting herself. Eyes glazed with desire looked at him, while her kiss-swollen lips parted.

"I . . . can't," he ground out.

Thea flattened her hands on the stones at her back and closed her eyes for a heartbeat. When she looked at him again, her eyes were clear once more.

He inwardly cringed when he spotted the hurt and distress there as she gazed at him. He'd known that kissing her would be a mistake. He'd realized it and yet condemned them both to the unending yearning for more.

Fisting his hands by his sides, he fought against the tide of longing, an ache so strong that he would surely feel it for eternity. Within him was a storm of emotions that he battled alone. They cut deeper, stung harder. The scars that would be left would be far more profound than the ones given by his wife.

How had he not sensed that Thea would have such an effect on him? Or had he known and sought the pleasure he knew he'd find in her arms anyway?

"I've never felt passion like that before." She gently pressed her lips together. "Have you?"

He slowly shook his head once. In fact, he didn't believe that such raging desire existed. Was this what his fellow Reapers had felt that caused them to court complete annihilation from Death? It had to be. Why else would they risk their existence?

They stared at each other. Eoghan struggled to remain where we was, while Thea simply waited. Long, long ago, Eoghan would've followed his heart. He would've thrown everything away just to be with her.

But that Eoghan no longer existed. He'd been destroyed, ripped apart piece by piece by his wife until she'd delivered the final, cruel blow.

He knew the instant one of his Reapers returned. The shift in the air alerted him, but it was also Thea's widening eyes. In some ways, Eoghan was glad that someone else was there. He had nothing left to say to Thea, but there was so much more he wanted to do to her. And his will was crumbling fast.

A second, then third Reaper appeared. Eoghan didn't turn to look behind him and see who had arrived. He couldn't take his eyes off Thea—or stop the longing within him.

He saw movement out of the corner of his eye. Aisling paused beside him. She cast him a quick glance before walking to Thea.

"Hey," Aisling said to her. "I'm sure you want to get home, but you should stay with us until we figure this out. I can get you anything you want. A hot bath?"

Thea pushed away from the wall and turned her head to Aisling. "I'd like that."

"Come with me." Aisling waited until Thea walked ahead of her before she glanced at Eoghan.

He gave her a nod of appreciation. Once the two had disappeared into one of the chambers, he turned to face the others. By this time, all the Reapers had returned.

"I suppose we should've knocked," Rordan said with a half-smile.

Cathal elbowed Rordan and shot him a stern frown.

Eoghan drew in a deep breath and released it. "Erith said you followed the Reapers around."

"Follow isn't the correct word," Dubhan said.

Bradach lifted one shoulder. "We weren't always there, but we did see some battles."

"We missed out on the one where Rhi was involved," Torin said. "I wished we would've seen that one."

Eoghan ran a hand down his face. "I asked that because I need to know how much all of you know about the others and their women."

"We know enough," Aisling said as she strode back into the center chamber. "Thea is soaking in a hot bath with some wine. I've also made it so she can't hear our conversation. Just in case you wanted to keep anything from her."

Eoghan bowed his head in thanks before addressing all of them. "Did Erith tell you the story of Bran?"

"She did," Dubhan replied.

Eoghan glanced at the arched ceiling above him. The paint was faded and chipping, but it must have been glorious at one time. "Each of the women with our fellow Reapers contributed to fighting Bran and this war we're in."

"You don't need to say more," Cathal declared. "We all intend to keep the vows we gave Death when she offered us our positions."

With that settled, Eoghan could turn his mind to other things. "Did any of you find anything at the cottage?"

"Two sets of tracks," Torin said. "One female, one male."

Bradach nodded. "Someone was there awhile. Male by the shoe size and depth of the tracks."

"So he didn't bother to hide his footprints?"

Torin issued a nonchalant shrug. "He did, and with some pretty powerful magic at that. But I was able to reveal them."

"Good job," Eoghan said.

Aisling sat on the overstuffed arm of one of the chairs. "Whoever wanted Thea hidden away went to great lengths to keep their identity secret."

"We need to find the one who hunted Thea," Rordan said. "That's how we'll find the answers."

Eoghan's gaze narrowed on Rordan. "You speak as if you know who it is."

"I've an idea."

"And?" Aisling asked with a loud sigh.

Rordan's nostrils flared as he glanced her way. "There has long been talk of a Fae banished from the Light. He can find anything you need. Some call him a Seeker. It's also said that he does business with both the Light and the Dark. He doesn't discriminate."

"Why was he banished?" Bradach asked.

Rordan shook his head. "I never heard that part of the tale."

"Do you have a name for this Seeker?" Eoghan asked.

"No, but I know how we can find him."

Eoghan contemplated that idea. He wanted to know if it was Bran after Thea, even as there was a part of him that knew it was a new enemy.

Dubhan crossed his arms over his chest. "I'll say what none of you have. We found the cottage too easily. Whoever veiled it, lowered their magic so Eoghan could find her."

"I know," Eoghan said.

Torin raised a black brow. "And you brought her back here?"

"It's the safest place," Aisling stated.

Eoghan ran a hand down his face, his mind sorting through the facts. "If it is this Seeker who kidnapped Thea, there's a chance he could know we're Reapers."

"How?" Bradach asked. "None of us have made it known."

"It's better to be prepared," Cathal stated.

Eoghan nodded in agreement. "Rordan, see if you can find this Fae. Use glamour to alter your face. Don't talk to him. Just locate him."

"Aye," Rordan said and teleported away.

Eoghan looked at the others. "Someone hired this Seeker to take Thea. We don't know if it's a Light or a Dark Fae."

"If a Dark wanted her, they would've taken her themselves," Dubhan said.

Cathal gave a nod of agreement. "True, but if they weren't sure where Thea was, they might have hired the Seeker. Still, once she was caught, why leave her in the cottage?"

"Thea did say someone was in there with her," Aisling said.

Eoghan got a sick feeling in his stomach. "Thea is an orphan. She never knew either of her parents. She was dropped off at a children's home when she was an infant."

"Oh," Aisling said with a frown.

Torin looked around. "What am I missing?"

Bradach said, "Eoghan thinks that it could be her Fae parent looking for her."

"Fek," Cathal said with a twist of his lips.

Dubhan grunted. "Well, if it was a female with the Seeker, that narrows down who we're looking for."

"It also points us to the Light," Torin replied.

Eoghan lowered his gaze to the ground. The magic within Thea was strong. It was rare in a Halfling with several generations of Fae blood flowing through him or her. Not so the case when one of the parents was a Fae.

"We're assuming the Fae after Thea is her mother," Torin said. "It could just be a woman working for the father. Think of how many mortal women put their children up for adoption."

Eoghan turned his gaze to Aisling. "We need more information on how Thea came to be at the children's home. Take Cathal and see what you two can find."

Once they were gone, Eoghan looked at the other three. "I put up wards around this level. Work your way up to the top with more. I want to know the moment another Fae comes close."

Now alone with Thea, Eoghan turned on his heel and looked at the door where she lounged in a tub on the other side. His emotions were still too raw to talk to her. Besides, he wanted information first.

CHAPTER
twelve

The cold seeping up through the stone floor didn't bother Thea as she rolled the empty wine bottle on its side. The bath had done wonders to relieve her tired muscles, but nothing could ease the ache within her except for Eoghan.

And he'd made it clear how he felt on that matter.

She still couldn't understand how someone could have such passion and ignore it. Or maybe he just didn't feel it as strongly she did.

Thea leaned back against the bed and closed her eyes. Aisling had given her all the comforts she could want. Thea had been awed by the magnitude of the female's magic.

While Aisling had been kind, Thea was all too aware that the Fae was part of Eoghan's group. A team he apparently led—a detail he'd left out.

Not that they had done a lot of talking. She knew very little about Eoghan, but still, she was drawn to him. It wasn't something she could ignore like Eoghan apparently could. But it would be handy to know his little trick for avoidance. Maybe then, she could get some sleep.

There were no windows in her room, and she had no way of knowing the time. She stifled a yawn. After being up for nearly forty-eight hours straight, her body wanted sleep.

She climbed into the bed and slid under the covers on her side. Her gaze was on the door, wondering what Eoghan was doing. She wished he'd come to her, but she knew he wouldn't. And that meant she couldn't—and wouldn't—go to him.

Her mind was too full of everything to allow her to find sleep. She rolled onto her back and put her hand on her forehead as she thought about her band and Annie. Did they even know she was gone?

She'd let it be known that she didn't like to talk on the phone and rarely texted. That made it so people rarely contacted her, which is exactly what she liked.

Or it was what she liked.

It was never clearer than at that moment that she had truly isolated herself from everyone. How many days would go by before Annie went to her flat?

She swiped at a tear. All her life, she'd felt as if she didn't belong. Even at the children's home where everyone was an orphan just like her. She always stood out, unable to fit in anywhere.

Nothing had changed as she grew older. It just became less of an issue. Even in her band, she didn't quite fit in. But the others didn't care, so it didn't matter to her.

She threw off the covers and rose from the bed. Her bare feet hit the stones, sending a chill through her. She ignored it as she walked to the door and opened it. Unsure where to go, she stood in the doorway and looked around.

Thea took a few steps toward the circular room at the center of the dwelling. She'd hoped Eoghan might be there. After a look in all the rooms, she discovered that she was alone.

It was how she normally preferred it, but now, she discovered she didn't want to be alone. She walked to one of the sofas and sat in the corner, tucking her legs against her. She was glad for the thick pajamas Aisling had given her.

She spotted her violin case, yet she didn't go to it. Odd since she it was never far from her.

The sound of approaching footsteps pulled her gaze away from her instrument. Her heart leapt at the sight of Eoghan. As soon as he saw her, he came to a halt.

"Is everything all right?" he asked.

She wrapped a hand around her cold toes. "Actually, I was hoping one of you might have found my mobile. I need to call Annie. She's my best friend."

"I know."

She frowned while trying to remember if Eoghan and Annie had met.

"I saw Annie at your flat."

Thea's back straightened, she was so taken aback. "Uh . . . what?"

"After I returned you to the pub, I found that I wanted to see you again."

"But you didn't know where I lived."

He shrugged as if to say it was no big deal. And for him, it wasn't because he was a Fae.

"When I was at your door, Annie arrived. She was frantic with worry."

Thea's heart warmed at the mention of her friend. "Really?"

"We searched your flat, and it took some convincing before she accepted that I wasn't a serial killer."

Thea laughed out loud. "Annie has an . . . well, I call it an obsession with serial killers and all movies and shows. Both documentaries and fiction. She's always telling me how a murderer could kill me since I take the same path home every time."

"She's a dedicated friend."

"Yes, she is," Thea said as she thought about Annie. "I need to let her know I'm okay."

"I agree. Especially since she's been shouting my name for the past hour."

"What?"

Eoghan sighed. "I promised I would go to her if she called for me."

"You told her what you are?"

"Of course, not."

Thea was confused. "And she accepted the fact that she could just say your name?"

"No, but she was willing to take a chance for you."

"Then why haven't you gone to her?"

Eoghan looked offended at her question. "I didn't want to leave you alone."

"It's probably better that you didn't. She's going to want to talk to me anyway."

Eoghan held out his hand, and a mobile phone appeared. He handed it to her. A part of Thea wanted to make sure their fingers touched, but she also couldn't be rejected a third time.

She took the phone and rose. "I'll go in my room so you won't have to hear the chatter."

"You think it bothers me?" he asked with a frown.

"I just assumed you'd rather be alone."

When he didn't reply, she turned and made her way to her room. Once the door was closed, she hastily dialed Annie's number.

As soon as her friend answered, Thea smiled. "Annie, it's me."

"Thea! Oh, my God. I've been so worried. What the hell happened to you? And why aren't you calling from your phone?"

"Mine is gone, but I'm fine."

Annie paused a moment then asked. "Who is Eoghan?"

"Someone I met the other night."

"He's a stunner, I'll give you that. But he's very . . . what's the word I'm looking for?"

"Reserved?" Thea suggested.

Annie snorted. "I was going to go with secretive, guarded. Cagey. Yes, cagey is a good word. Care to tell me how he just disappeared? I'd like to know that trick."

"He's the one who found me," Thea stated.

"Did he?" Annie whispered in shock. "I wasn't sure if he would. I mean, he certainly looked capable and all that, but I was about to head to the authorities to file a missing person report."

Thea walked to the bed and fell back onto the mattress before tucking her feet beneath the covers. "Thank you for caring."

"I know you may not believe this, but people do care about you."

"I'm learning that. I'm so sorry for being such a pain."

"Come over, and we can talk about it as well as Mr. Cagey."

Thea closed her eyes. "I wish I could."

"What's going on?"

"I can't tell you all of it, at least not now. Once it's over, I will. But someone kidnapped me. I don't know why. Eoghan found me, and I'll be with him as we figure things out."

"Damn," Annie murmured.

Thea thought of all the times she'd brushed Annie off and felt a pang of regret. She swept aside a tear that fell down her cheek.

"What do you need from me?" her friend asked.

Thea opened her eyes and looked at the far wall. "Nothing. Just go on as usual."

"What about the band?"

"I don't know how long this could take. Replace me if you have to."

Annie laughed dryly. "Ah. No. I'll tell the others an emergency came up. Can I contact you through this number?"

"I think so."

"Well, there's so much more I want to say and ask, but you sound exhausted. Get some sleep. Check in when you can."

Thea smiled. "Thanks, Annie. And thanks for not freaking out on me."

"Oh, honey. I freaked. I'm still freaking. Trust me. You'll get a dose when I see you."

The line disconnected. Thea laid the mobile next to her pillow as she turned onto her side and pulled up the covers. This time when she closed her eyes, she felt sleep pulling at her.

Eoghan stood outside Thea's door. He hadn't wanted to listen in on her conversation, but he'd needed to know how she was really feeling, and she would only tell Annie that.

He left his spot when Bradach returned and walked into the main room. The Light Fae lowered himself into one of the chairs before crossing an ankle over his knee.

Eoghan studied the Reaper. "I know you wanted to be one of us. I also know you can fight. Why do you hide it?"

Bradach drew in a deep breath and slowly released it as he ran a hand through his short hair. "Probably for the same reason you're trying to pretend that you wouldn't do anything just to have Thea in your arms."

Eoghan sat in the spot she'd recently occupied on the sofa. "I watched Bran fall in love and try to have something that could never be his. It turned him into a monster. He divided us and turned Reaper against Reaper."

"But the others in Cael's group are fine. Death has accepted the women. I also know that Death has rescinded her rule about not having relationships."

"I know firsthand how Cael and the others are bending over backwards to keep the Halflings safe. If Bran could get his hands on them, he would."

"And you don't want your attention divided," Bradach said.

Eoghan shook his head. "It's too late for me. But it's also why I know that this isn't the life for Thea."

"I agree with you a hundred percent. But you didn't see your face when we returned. We all knew the two of you were kissing. The need was palpable."

"Bran wants to kill me. He's after our brethren and Erith. I'm ready to die for them—for you—so he doesn't win. If I give in to the desire and take Thea, I'll compromise myself."

Bradach lowered his foot to the ground and sat forward, resting his arms on his legs. "Do you really think any of us would allow Bran to get to Thea?"

"I know you would try, but there again is the conflict. Our mission isn't to protect Halflings. We're Reapers. We take those Death has judged."

"Then what did you and your team do for the past few months? You saved Halflings. Hundreds of them, in fact."

Eoghan looked away because Bradach had a point. It felt as if everything and everyone were pushing him to succumb to his desire. But he feared it. Mostly, he worried what he might become if he opened that part of himself again.

The problem was that Thea had cracked that door open the moment she looked up at him after pulling him from the portal stones. And every time he had been with her after that, the door was pushed wider and wider.

The kiss had kicked it all the way open.

"Do you know what I would do if I had such a gift before me?" Bradach asked.

Eoghan's gaze slid to him. He looked into the Fae's silver eyes. "Aye, I do."

"So, you know my past? You know why I'm a Reaper?"

"I do," Eoghan replied.

Bradach pushed to his feet. "Then don't be a fool and make my same mistakes."

CHAPTER
thirteen

t was amazing what fifteen hours of sleep could do. Thea stretched and yawned before she rose from the warmth of the bed. The cool air brushing against her shook off any vestiges of slumber.

She grinned when she saw the rack against the wall, full of black clothes and lingerie. Aisling must have done it while she slept. Thea looked through the various pants, shirts, and jackets before choosing a pair of black jeans and a black, long-sleeved, collared shirt with a low V in the front. She liked the texture of the shirt and the way it skimmed her figure.

Thea then put on her boots before combing her fingers through her hair. It was a tangled mess, so instead of fighting it, she threw it up into a messy updo at the back of her head. Aisling had even supplied a toothbrush and toothpaste that Thea gladly took advantage of.

The Dark Fae had thought of everything. Thea needed to do

more than simply say "thank you." But how did one show appreciation to a Fae who had magic to get anything they wanted?

At the door, Thea drew a deep breath to ready herself before opening it. As soon as she stepped out, her gaze immediately found Eoghan.

He halted in the middle of speaking when he saw her. All seven of them shifted their eyes to her. It was disconcerting, to say the least. Yet she refused to let it get to her. She held Eoghan's gaze, not quite sure what to do.

"How do you feel?" he asked.

Thea felt her muscles relax at his words. "Better."

"Come meet the others," he bade.

As if she would pass up such an offer. She walked to stand beside him and faced the six Fae. How different her life was now. She was in a room full of gorgeous beings with magic.

"You already know Aisling," Eoghan said as he started on the left.

Thea smiled at the Fae. "Thank you for the clothes."

"My pleasure," Aisling said with a wink.

Eoghan then motioned to the man beside her. "That is Bradach."

Thea looked into the Light's silver eyes and grinned. Next up was Dubhan, and then Torin. At the end was Rordan, and the giant, Cathal.

After the introductions, the room grew uncomfortably silent. Thea blew out a breath and turned to Eoghan. "Should I leave so you can get back to what I obviously interrupted?"

"We were discussing you," Eoghan said. His quicksilver eyes swung to her. Then he told the others, "We need a moment."

Just like that, the six vanished. No questions, no arguments. Just complete obedience. Thea confirmed that Eoghan was in charge after seeing him with the group, but he didn't seem to carry the mantle easily.

"Discussing me, huh?" she asked with a forced grin. "It must be something terrible for you to have that stern look."

Eoghan frowned before shaking his head. "Forgive me. I'm handling this badly."

"Who are you? I know your name, but little else."

He glanced at the ground. "You know more about me than most."

"So you keep people at a distance, as well, huh?"

"I've mastered the art."

She grinned at his words. "I understand. I won't ask any more questions."

"Ask. Please."

His request shocked her to the point that her mind went blank. Then the questions jumbled in her head like one huge ball.

She walked past him to the sofa and sat. He turned to watch before sinking into the chair nearest her. She wished he had sat beside her, but at least he was close.

"You asked who we are," Eoghan said before she could repeat the question. "As a Halfling, you know nothing about Fae culture. The Light and Dark have been at war for as long as I can remember."

"And how long is that?" she interjected.

His chest expanded as he inhaled. "I'm nearing nine thousand years."

Her mouth fell open. "You're immortal."

"No. We just live a really long time, but we can be killed."

She looked at Eoghan with new eyes.

"There is a legend among the Fae about Reapers. It's nothing like what mortals consider. Reapers to a Fae are like your fairytales. Both the Dark and Light use the Reapers to ensure that their children do what they are told."

"Okay," she said, waiting for him to continue.

"Reapers are real. I know this because I'm one of them. So are the six under my command."

Thea blinked and nodded. What else was she supposed to say?

Eoghan continued, either not noticing her reaction, or preferring not to mention it. "Death finds us after we die. Each of us went through a betrayal that led to our deaths, but more than that, we were—are—each warriors in our own right."

"You died?" she asked in confusion.

He issued a single nod. "Death is judge and jury to the Fae. The Reapers are the executioners. No Fae can know who we are. If they find out, they're killed."

Thea sat up straighter, not at all liking the idea of her life being snuffed out for such knowledge. "And me?"

"Death doesn't hold Halflings to the same standards. At least not any who don't have a connection to the Fae."

"Oh." That made her feel marginally better. "A Reaper, huh?"

His mercurial eyes slid away to look at the distant wall. "Once we accept the offer to join the Reapers, we belong to Death. Our magic is increased, and we become stronger and faster than any other Fae."

"How long are you in service to Death?"

"For eternity," he replied, returning his gaze to her. "Or until we're killed again."

She frowned. "Death brings you back but allows you to be killed again? That doesn't seem fair."

"There are limits to all magic. Even for someone like Death."

"And you lead them."

"I lead this group, yes."

Her eyes widened. "There are more?"

"Yes."

She was about to ask how many groups when Eoghan surprised her with a question.

"Did you ever look for your birth parents?"

Thea shook her head. "There was a time when it was all I thought about, but I was only a teenager and didn't have the funds. I did ask those at the children's home where I lived, but they said they didn't have anything to point me in the right direction."

"Did you believe them?"

She cocked her head at him. "What aren't you telling me?"

"I sent Aisling and Cathal to dig into the records of the place you grew up."

When Eoghan didn't continue, she raised her brows. "And? You can't just leave me hanging like that. What did they find?"

"The building burned last night."

Thea felt as if she'd been punched, the shock was so great. "What?"

"Aisling and Cathal got there in time to see the last part of the building collapse. They remained veiled and walked among the mortals to see if there was a Fae among them, but they found nothing."

"Veiled?" she asked, grasping at something that she would get an answer to.

Eoghan rested his limbs on the arms of the chair. "All Fae can veil themselves to keep hidden from humans as well as other Fae. As Reapers, we can see any Fae who tries to veil themselves, but they can't see us."

She put her hand on her stomach and realized that she was breathing heavily. "I never liked the children's home. They were decent to me, but it wasn't where I belonged. Yet, I never wanted it destroyed. Was anyone hurt?"

"All the children were evacuated. One woman, a Ms. Fylan, died from smoke inhalation."

Thea got to her feet and began to pace. She realized she was wringing her hands, and she immediately went into her room to get her violin. She carried the instrument back out to Eoghan.

"It was Ms. Fylan who thought music might help me. She put this violin into my hands and taught me to play. She was a sweet woman who adored children. Of all the people to have been killed, why did it have to be her?"

Eoghan nodded at the instrument. "Play, Thea."

"What?" she asked in confusion.

"Look at your fingers."

She looked down to find the first two fingers of her left hand moving just above the strings without touching them. Her gaze skated back to Eoghan, who merely waited.

As soon as she'd brought the violin to her shoulder and placed the bow on the strings, she was able to breathe easier. The music that flowed from her was rapid and brisk. The bow moved at such speed that it became a blur.

All the chaos, all the uncertainty that she'd been burying poured from her as if a dam had been broken. The emotions cascaded from her like an endless faucet. The more she played, the more she thought about her kidnapping and her parents. And the more agitated she became.

Until suddenly, there was no more music.

Her bow halted on the strings, the last note fading away. She lifted the bow, but she couldn't move more than that. Then a large hand wrapped around hers. She felt Eoghan come up behind her and loop his arm around her waist as he held her.

She leaned her head back against him and drew in a shuddering breath. How many years of emotions had she finally released? She felt . . . not exactly free, but lighter. As if her worries had been cut in half.

"It's going to be all right," he whispered.

"Is it? I don't even know what's going on."

His arm tightened around her. "I'll be right here beside you. We'll do this together."

She lowered the arm holding the violin. "Can you do that? Will Death let you?"

"The Reapers have saved hundreds of Halflings recently. I can —and will—save you."

"Thank you."

She closed her eyes and savored the feeling of his arms around her, of his strength holding her. Her stomach fluttered in excitement when he rested his head against hers.

"Someone set the fire, didn't they?" she asked.

Eoghan released a breath. "It could be a coincidence."

"But you don't believe so."

"No, I don't. The fact that it happened right after you were taken raises concerns."

She lifted her head as fear began to grow within her. "Do you think the ones who wanted me kidnapped know I'm gone?"

"I've sent Rordan to find the man he believes took you. If we can locate him and get some answers, I believe we'll discover why he let us find you."

Thea spun around and searched Eoghan's face, still encircled in his arms. "Why would he do that after going to so much trouble to take me?"

"That's something I intend to find out."

"I know what he looks like. I want to help search for him."

Eoghan began shaking his head before she'd finished speaking. "Absolutely not."

"You'll be by my side the entire time."

His lips parted before he closed his mouth and stared at her. After a moment, he said, "We'll be at the Dark Palace. Surrounded by them."

"Aisling is Dark. And so are Cathal and Dubhan."

"When a Fae becomes a Reaper, we retain the appearance of who we were, but we're no longer the same. While Aisling, Dubhan, and Cathal have the coloring of a Dark, they no longer have those tendencies. You won't be prepared for what you'll see at the palace."

She lifted her chin. "Does Rordan know what the Fae looks like?"

"No," Eoghan said after a small hesitation.

"We want answers. I'm your quickest way to gaining them."

"He could've used glamour to hide his face."

She smiled, her confidence growing. "Maybe. But no one can pick out voices like I can."

"So be it."

CHAPTER
fourteen

"This is so cool," Thea said as she looked at her reflection.

Eoghan stood in the doorway to her room, watching her. He couldn't stop the worry that continued to spread after he'd agreed to bring Thea into the Dark Palace to hunt for the Seeker.

She tossed her black and silver hair back and forth with a shake of her head. She leaned close to the mirror and looked at her red eyes. Eoghan didn't alter anything else about her except for hiding her nose ring.

"How long will this last?" Thea asked as she turned to him.

Eoghan shrugged. "As long as I want it to."

"Do I need to change?"

"Oh, you'll fit right in with the all black," Aisling said as she walked to stand beside Eoghan. She turned her head and gave him a look filled with concern. "Tell me this is just you passing the time. Tell me you aren't seriously going to put her in the palace?"

Eoghan turned to Aisling before he glanced at Thea inside her chamber. "She's the only one who knows what the Seeker looks like. And, in case he used glamour, she can pick out his voice."

"If you're going in, then we all go," Aisling stated firmly.

He had worried about having a female Reaper since he hadn't exactly been around a lot of women over the years, but out of all of his Reapers, Aisling was the one most willing to work as a team. She was spirited and wore her anger over her betrayal like a shield.

But she was as loyal as they came. Out of all of his Reapers, what happened to Aisling was the most heinous. Eoghan would have wanted Aisling as a Reaper even if Death hadn't chosen her.

He gave her a nod.

"We're all going where?" Torin asked as he and the others strode in.

Thea smiled as she came to stand beside Eoghan. "We're going to the Dark Palace."

Eoghan watched the faces of his Reapers, emotions that ranged from surprise to eagerness to admiration to incredulity. He knew that it would only take a few minutes in the Dark Palace for Thea's excitement to dim. She wanted to help, but if there were another way to find the Seeker without her, Eoghan would do it.

"I've spoken to Rordan. In the day that he's been gone, he's found nothing of the Seeker. No one has seen the Fae in months," Eoghan said.

Bradach asked, "Could he be at the Light Castle?"

"We'll have to search there, as well." Eoghan blew out a breath. "Whether I like it or not, Thea may be able to help us. She knows the Seeker's face. And his voice. Unless we want to devote weeks or months to this, we have to use her."

Dubhan shook his head. "It's a mistake bringing her to the Dark."

"It's why we're all going," Aisling said.

Cathal gave a nod of agreement. "Good."

Eoghan looked at Thea, wondering if she were the very thing helping to bring his Reapers together. She looked at him with her red eyes and smiled in encouragement.

"I've already alerted Rordan that we're coming," Eoghan continued. "We need to split up. Just as I ordered Rordan, alter everything about your appearance. Cathal, even your height."

One after another, the Reapers changed their faces, clothes, hair, eyes, and bodies. Eoghan gave Thea time to get used to their new looks before he sent them off.

"Why aren't we leaving?" she asked.

He faced her and took her hand. "Listen to me closely. You're likely to see one of them doing something that is hard to accept. In order to fit in, my Reapers will become Dark."

"I understand."

"I'm not sure you do." He ran a hand down his face. "Remember when I said the Dark consume human souls through sex?"

Thea nodded, a frown furrowing her brows as she listened.

"There will be humans there. Some will be dead and dying—all with smiles on their faces. The others will be enthralled with the Fae, reaching out to them for the pleasure they'll receive. But occasionally, there will be one who resists, one who screams for help."

Thea's features tightened with alarm. "And you want me to know that we can't help any of those people."

"Yes. You can't even take notice of them. If you do, it'll draw attention."

She squared her shoulders. "I can do this. I won't let you down."

He was taken aback by her words. "It takes a lot of courage to do what you're about to do. I tell you all of this not because I don't want you to fail, but because I'm concerned about how this will affect you."

"I need to do this."

Eoghan held out his hand. "If you're sure."

She put her hand in his and held his gaze. "Let's go find this jerk."

There was a smile on his face when he teleported them outside of the Dark Palace. Dusk was upon them, with night fast approaching.

"There's nothing here," Thea whispered.

Eoghan faced the palace. "Close your eyes. Your human side is preventing you from seeing what is right before you." He looked over to see if she was doing as he asked. "Good. Now, open your other senses. The magic is there, waiting for you to feel it."

Her head tilted to the side as her brow creased in concentration. "I feel . . . something. It's like it's pushing back against me. It doesn't hurt. In fact, it feels good."

"Magic," he said.

Her brow smoothed as she smiled. "I want to feel more of it."

"First, see it," he urged.

He watched as her lids opened, and her eyes widened. Then she looked at him with a huge smile. There was no need to ask if she saw the palace. The evidence was there for him to witness.

She was easily the most beautiful thing he'd ever seen. When he thought about what might have become of her if he hadn't gone to see her at the pub that night, his stomach knotted painfully.

And if he hadn't wanted to talk to her after Egpyt, he might never have known she was missing. It didn't matter who'd kidnapped her or why. He was going to make sure she was never harmed again.

While he was gazing at her like a love-struck fool, Thea was studying the Dark Palace.

"I expected more," she replied with a frown. "It's just so . . . dark and gloomy. It's a magnificent structure, I suppose."

He looked down at their still clasped hands. "If you want grandeur, then you need to see the Light Castle."

"I'd love to."

Eoghan chuckled. "Shall we go inside?"

"As soon as I drop the veil, everyone will be able to see us."

"I'm ready."

She might be, but he wasn't. And never would be. Going into the palace was akin to walking into a viper's nest. There was a guarantee that you would get bitten. It was just a matter of anticipating the strike and averting as much as possible.

"Here we go," he said and dropped the veil.

He pulled her after him as he walked to the entrance. The tall, wide double doors were arched and decorated with iron similar to most castle entrances.

"There are no guards," Thea murmured.

Eoghan pushed open the doors and stepped inside. "Why would there be? The Dark don't care if you come in. No Light would willingly come here. Most mortals will sense the veil around it and leave, but there are those who venture inside. The Dark eagerly welcome them. And as for other Dark, this is a gathering place."

"I see," she said.

He paused inside the doors. "Still sure you want to go on?"

"Definitely," she stated with a nod.

Eoghan looked over his shoulder out the door. Then he faced

forward again and began walking through the crowd of Dark. For her part, Thea kept her gaze straight ahead. Her breathing had quickened, however. And she gripped his hand as if it were her life support.

"Doing good," he told her.

She shot him a grateful look. "Where are we going? This place is huge, and there are Fae everywhere."

"In case you haven't noticed, I'm taking you near any groups so you can listen to voices."

"Oh. I hadn't."

He gave her hand a reassuring squeeze and walked them into one of the vast halls where some Dark gathered. Pillows of all colors and sizes littered the floor where the Fae reclined. There were enclosures throughout the hall that resembled giant bird-cages, and within were mortals.

Eoghan halted when they were relatively alone. He pushed Thea against a wall and caught her gaze as he moved in front of her. "Look at me. That's it, get your bearings again."

"You warned me," she whispered.

He flattened his lips. "No descriptions could prepare anyone for this."

"Doesn't anyone realize how many humans go missing?"

"There are several billion people on this planet. Few notice when someone disappears."

"I know."

"Forget the mortals. You need to look around the room, listen to voices."

She shot him a look of outrage. "In case you missed it, this room is massive. And dark. The lighting sucks. It would take me hours to look at each face."

"Forget the women. Concentrate on the men."

"Sometimes, it's hard to tell from behind. Some of the men have longer hair than the women."

Whatever Eoghan had been about to say flew from his mind when her hands slid into his hair. He put a hand on the wall next to her head in an attempt to hold himself away.

But her fingers felt so good combing through his length. He'd left it down and loose of any braids, which allowed her free rein. She took it, too, as she lightly scraped his scalp from his temples down to his neck.

It caused chills to rise on his skin. He leaned closer, seeking more of her attention. All the while, their eyes were locked.

Of all the times for him to lose control, this was not the place to do it. But he was powerless to resist—not to mention, he didn't want to fight Thea's allure.

Bradach's words from the day before continued to drift through this mind, warring with the part of him that knew it was folly to surrender.

"You look at me as if you want nothing else but me," Thea said.

His gaze dropped to her mouth. He remembered how sweet she tasted, how perfect she felt in his arms.

"But you push me away." Her nails slid over his neck to his chest. "I've never known anyone with your strength of will before."

"Th—

"Eoghan."

Eoghan jerked when he heard Rordan call his name. He pushed away from the wall and looked around the room.

"What is it?" Thea questioned.

"Rordan just said my name. It was done as a warning," he explained.

Thea's gaze darted around. "About what?"

Eoghan's did a double-take when he spotted Rhi. The Light Fae was veiled and reclining on an archway about thirty feet above Balladyn. Rhi swung her feet like a child while she looked at Balladyn with murder in her eyes.

For his part, the new King of the Dark seemed distracted as he looked around as if searching for someone.

"What is it?" Thea asked.

Eoghan smiled. "Someone who can help."

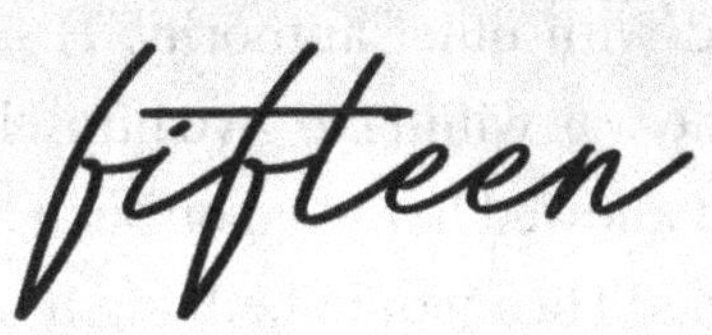

fifteen

While caught in a palace of killers, there was only one who ensnared Thea's attention. Eoghan. Even with his glamour that turned his eyes a vivid red and the thick silver streaks in his midnight locks, he was still the most gorgeous, magnificent man she had ever laid eyes on.

Or ever would.

There wasn't a single being in all the worlds that could compare to him. While some might find his solemn, serious nature a drawback, she thought it sexy. Or maybe that was because he was one of those rare individuals who would rush into the most extreme danger to save others without regard for themselves.

It was no wonder Death wanted him for a Reaper. Eoghan was strong, courageous, and powerful. His intense, deep-rooted sense of justice made him stand out from all others. He was a survivor, as was evident by his betrayal and subsequent death, and then the hellish world he'd pulled himself from.

Such things would've broken lesser men. Instead, it had only added to Eoghan's strength, making him a dangerous enemy—and a powerful ally.

In the little time she had been around the Reapers, she'd seen how he commanded with quiet authority. He expected no more from his team than he was willing to give himself.

The fact that he'd allowed her to go on such a mission said a lot about the man he was. Thea would be lying if she said she wasn't terrified, but if there were anyone who could keep her safe, it was Eoghan.

She was supposed to be looking and listening for the Fae who'd kidnapped her, but her attention kept returning to Eoghan. If only they were alone. If only he would kiss her again.

Thea frowned as his worry penetrated the haze of her desire. "You see someone who can help?"

"Maybe," Eoghan murmured, his attention directed elsewhere.

She mourned the loss of their semi-seclusion. There might be a thousand Dark around them, but for just a few minutes, there had only been the two of them.

"Good," she said. "Do you want to go talk to them?"

"We will," Eoghan murmured as his brow furrowed.

Thea turned her head to the side to take a look at the Fae surrounding them as she was supposed to. Her gaze ran over several faces before her eyes jerked back to a man standing off by himself in a corner. His attention was locked on two Dark deep in conversation.

She tapped Eoghan's arm, not taking her gaze from the Fae for fear of losing him. When Eoghan didn't immediately respond, she hit him harder.

"Um . . . Eoghan. I found him," she said.

Instantly, Eoghan's gaze was on her before turning to where she looked. "Which one?"

"The one by himself."

"Are you sure?"

"Positive. He didn't change his appearance."

Eoghan glanced at whoever he thought could help. "I've alerted the others. Talking to him here is a bad idea. Too many Dark."

"He'd follow me if he could see my real face."

"No," Eoghan stated.

She looked to Eoghan. "We need answers. I need answers. We don't want an incident where we call attention to ourselves. But I might be able to lead him out of here to somewhere more private."

He stared at her a long minute. "If I agree to this, I'll be beside you veiled the entire time."

"I'd want it no other way," she stated. "I might want answers, but I've no wish to be caught by anyone here."

Eoghan's lips flattened as his gaze slid away. "Aisling and Dubhan will also be veiled while the others station themselves elsewhere. There is statuary out back. It's a good place to talk since few are out there."

"Okay," she said, reservations rushing through her now that Eoghan had agreed.

His eyes snapped back to her. "I'll lead you there, but it'll be up to you to get the Fae to follow."

"I understand," she stated."

He hesitated, then said, "I'll be beside you the entire time with my hand on your arm to help guide you."

"How do you know this place so well?"

"The Reapers have been here many times for those Death has judged."

Thea nodded. "Ah. Right."

Eoghan blew out a harsh breath. "Ready?"

"As I'll ever be," she replied.

She missed his nearness the moment he stepped away. He gave her a nod and said, "I'll be right back."

Though Eoghan was only gone for a matter of seconds, Thea had never felt so exposed. She imagined that every Dark was now staring at her.

She sagged against the wall when an invisible hand touched her arm. Eoghan. Thank God he was back, even if he was now veiled. Since this was her idea, there was no backing out now. Besides, she wanted answers.

"I'm ready when you are," Eoghan said from beside her.

His disembodied voice reassured her. Thea pushed away from the wall and made her way to the Fae. She was almost upon him before his red eyes swung to her. Thanks to Eoghan's glamour, there was nothing about her the Fae recognized.

"Can I help you?" he asked, not bothering to keep the irritation from his voice.

She stood beside him and looked at the men he'd been staring at. "Thinking of kidnapping someone else?"

That's all it took for his attention to land squarely on her. "Do I know you?"

"You would if I didn't look like this. It was only a few days ago that I got out of the cottage you locked me in."

"Thea?" he whispered in shock. "What the holy fek are you doing here?"

"Looking for you."

His eyes lifted and scanned the room with narrowed eyes. "Who else is with you?"

"Some friends. But you don't need to concern yourself with them." She was proud of how commanding her voice sounded. "How about we talk somewhere more private?"

His red eyes slid to her, and he stared for a long minute. "And if I don't want to?"

"You really want to."

"Now isn't a good time."

She shrugged. "It wasn't exactly a good time when you took me from the street either, but you didn't care about that."

His nostrils flared. "Fine. Let's get this over with."

Thea turned in the direction Eoghan tugged her. She and the Dark didn't utter another word as they walked side by side from the room and through a labyrinth of corridors until she spotted a doorway.

She continued walking out onto the veranda and down the steps to the statues below. There were dozens of them, some naked, some clothed, but all modeled after Fae—if their beauty was any indication. Thea did a double-take as she looked at a statue that was a replica of David.

As soon as she was outside, she drew in a breath to steady herself. Being outdoors and away from so many Dark made her feel better.

The Fae snorted as he came to a stop. "Being out here is no different than inside those doors. You should remember that."

Thea faced him and glared. She didn't know how long she had before Eoghan and the others made themselves known. "Why did you take me?" she demanded.

"It was a job."

"Who wanted me kidnapped?"

The Dark folded his arms over his chest and looked around. "I know you're not alone."

"Answer my question."

"Not until the others show themselves."

No sooner had the words left his mouth than Eoghan dropped

his veil. The other six then did the same. The Fae looked at each of them before his gaze halted on Eoghan.

"Give her the answer," Eoghan ordered.

Thea waited anxiously, but the seconds ticked by with only silence.

Cathal took a menacing step toward the Dark. "You were given a command."

The Fae glanced at Cathal and smiled. "I'm not afraid of you."

"You should be," Dubhan stated.

The Fae and Eoghan stared at each other, neither moving. Thea looked at Aisling, who gave a shake of her head, warning Thea to remain silent.

Thea stared at the Fae, trying to understand why he didn't fear the seven surrounding him. And that's when it hit her.

"You're more afraid of who paid you to take me," she said.

There was the slightest twitch in the Dark's countenance to prove that her theory was correct.

"You've got it wrong," Bradach told the Dark. "You should be more afraid of us."

The Fae snorted. "I know who you are—or rather what you are."

"That's impossible," Torin said.

Eoghan took a step closer to the Fae. "Who are you?"

"If you're going to kill me, do it," the Dark stated. "Otherwise, let me go so I can finish what I began."

"Another victim waiting to be kidnapped?" Rordan quipped.

The Fae turned his head and speared Rordan with a hard look. "No."

"But you're the one they call the Seeker, aren't you?" Eoghan asked.

The Dark swung his head back to Eoghan and gave a brief nod of his head. "I am. Now, get on with the killing."

A sword appeared in Dubhan's hand, but he didn't advance on the Dark. Instead, he waited for Eoghan's order. Thea looked at the group. Curiously, the only one who hadn't spoken was Aisling.

"Wait," Thea said as she moved to stand between Eoghan and the Fae.

Eoghan's gaze lowered to her with a frown. "You would protect him after what he did to you?"

"He never harmed me. He took me against my will, yes, but that was all." She licked her lips, searching for the right words. "I've gone my entire life without knowing anything. If he holds even one answer, then I ask that you don't kill him. Yet."

"That's not up to us," Aisling said.

Thea turned to find the Dark staring at Aisling, but she wouldn't look at him.

Then the Fae swiveled his head toward Thea. "Be wary. The one who wants you will be after you again."

"Who is it?" Thea implored.

The Dark's lips thinned as he inhaled. "A very powerful Fae."

"You need to give us more than that," Eoghan said.

The Dark shook his head. "I've got one chance to come out of this alive, and you're ruining it."

"So, you did allow me to find her." Eoghan reached for Thea's hand and drew her beside him.

"I did."

Thea was taken aback by the admission. "Why?"

"I've my reasons."

Bradach said, "Whoever hired you, pissed you off. It's your way of getting back."

"If the Fae is as powerful as he says, why isn't he worried?" Torin asked.

Eoghan raised a brow. "Good question."

The Dark shook his head, a small smile playing about his lips. "That it is."

"How about you answer it," Cathal demanded, a warning in his voice.

The Fae shrugged indifferently, looking bored with the entire encounter. But Thea suspected that it was just for show. She could be wrong, but what would it hurt to see?

"You didn't have to take the job to kidnap me," she said. The Fae's red eyes slid to her. "You also didn't have to let me go. If the one who wanted me taken is so powerful, I'm guessing you were getting something pretty important for accepting the job."

"Or you wanted something," Eoghan added.

The Dark grinned as he looked at Eoghan. "You'd better be on your toes, Reaper. Because the one who wants Thea will stop at nothing to have her."

No sooner had the last word fallen from his lips than he vanished.

"You've got to be fekking kidding me," Rordan replied angrily.

Thea looked around in confusion. "What's the problem?"

"We were preventing him from leaving," Aisling said. "Or so we thought."

Eoghan took Thea's hand and told the others, "Return to the base."

CHAPTER

sixteen

Xaneth hated being taken by surprise. He'd made it his life's work ensuring that didn't happen. Never in his wildest dreams did he think the Reapers would be able to find him, mostly because they had no idea what he looked like.

That was the reason he hadn't altered his facial structure. If he'd had even a hint that the Reapers would bring Thea to the Dark Palace, he would've taken the appropriate steps.

And he'd been so close to finding someone who would take him to Bran.

Then Thea had to go and ruin it.

He teleported to the ruins of an old Irish castle and squatted on his haunches with his back against a wall while he tried to sort out the most recent mess.

The longer Xaneth remained without Bran's assistance, the easier it would be for Usaeil to find him. When she did locate him . . . it would be game over. The hope that had kept him going all these centuries would be destroyed, much like his family had been.

And now that the queen knew of his existence, she wouldn't allow him to live regardless. There was much the Light didn't know about Usaeil.

If only he hadn't tried to reach for the impossible. He'd made a good life for himself. Well, good might be the wrong term. Decent was more like it.

He had friends in both the Dark and Light. There were many who owed him favors, and more that were willing to help him. He was respected, and in some cases, even feared.

And he'd thrown it all away just because he wanted to go home. Everyone in his family had been killed to ensure there was no one left.

Then he'd gone and let Usaeil know that he was still alive.

"Great fekking thinking," he growled to himself.

Xaneth squeezed his eyes closed and propped his forehead on his hands. He knew his magic exceeded most of the Fae's, but he wasn't sure about going up against Usaeil. Yet, he may have no other choice.

He dropped his head back on the wall and opened his eyes to the night sky above him through the busted roof. A simple life with simple pleasures had been his for the taking. It had been in his grasp. Now, even that was gone.

And to make matters worse, he just had to show off and alert the Reapers that he knew who they were.

He never made such horrible decisions. What was wrong with him? But he knew. The possibility of having the banishment reversed and his family's name once more spoken with pride had been too much for him to resist.

The last time he'd done something so stupid, it had gotten his little sister killed. This time, he would forfeit his own life.

Who would find him first? Death? The Reapers? Or Usaeil?

He really hoped it wasn't the Light Queen. If he couldn't win, at least he could make sure that she didn't get to take his life. It would be a small victory.

If only he could've found Bran. He didn't know or care what the Fae was doing building an army. It was enough that Bran might have the means to kill Usaeil.

"Shite," he mumbled.

In his quest for vengeance, not once had he thought what might become of the Light. If Bran was as powerful as he'd heard whispered, then with an army at his back, he might wipe out the Light entirely.

But one problem at a time. Right now, Xaneth had to find a way to stay alive—and stop making enemies. The only solution was Bran.

He blew out a breath and stood. The palace had been the perfect place for him to get to Bran, but he couldn't chance returning with the Reapers there. Which meant he needed to find another place where the Dark gathered.

He teleported to Cork.

Erith wanted nothing more than to give Xaneth the information he wanted. She could point him in Bran's direction. But Xaneth was a Fae who didn't see the lines between Light and Dark—through no fault of his own.

Because of his family's banishment, they'd learned to live in harmony on the outskirts of both worlds. It was a feat no one else had ever accomplished.

In truth, it was Xaneth who'd managed such an accomplishment, not his family. Yet he made sure everyone he loved was included in the pacts and truces he made.

She had been watching him for some time. Despite the betrayal of his family, he still managed to live life to the very fullest. He had his moments of melancholy, but he never allowed them to last long.

He was a Fae who could truly judge both the Light and the Dark impartially. He didn't hold the Light responsible for his banishment any more than he did the Dark. He knew the blame lay squarely with Usaeil.

If only it were as easy as sending out judgment for the queen—which in fact, Erith had done a millennia ago. But things worked differently with those in power.

So, while Erith wouldn't send a Reaper to claim Usaeil's soul, she could go herself. If only she weren't so weak, she'd do just that. She should've done it years ago, but there was someone who caused her to hesitate, one who showed great promise. One who could alter things. That was why she hadn't already claimed Usaeil's soul.

Erith knew by her rules that Xaneth should be killed for knowing who the Reapers were, but she withheld her decision. He could be an asset—if he didn't help Bran annihilate the Light.

She even contemplated telling Xaneth everything to see if she could turn him to her side. But she'd decided against it at the last moment.

Xaneth was the one player in the game who couldn't be manipulated. He was too strong—mentally and physically. Ultimately,

Xaneth could be the one to change everything. If only she had seen it sooner, she would have reached out to him.

It was a mistake that could cost her everything. And it was just the beginning of what Bran would do to the inhabitants of Earth.

Eoghan sent his team out to scour Ireland and both the Light and Dark courts for any information on the Seeker. He paced his chamber, desperately trying not to think of the fact that he was alone with Thea.

Once they'd returned from the Dark Palace, he removed the glamour on both himself and her. Her disappointment in learning nothing was palpable. He felt it himself, but his anger pushed it aside.

How in the bloody hell had the Seeker managed to teleport away when he and the others were using their magic to ensure that he couldn't? Only someone with immense power could do that.

Those who had more magic than Reapers were rare. It would help to narrow down who this Fae was, but that couldn't happen fast enough.

Eoghan tried to keep his mind occupied, but all he could think about was Thea. The more he fought the desire, the more it grew.

Finally, he strode from his chamber and crossed the rotunda to Thea's door. He gripped the sides of the frame and attempted once more to get control of himself.

But it was a half-hearted endeavor. Thea was in his soul, on his skin, and buried in his psyche. No amount of denial would change that.

He closed his eyes, wondering what it was about her that made him so weak? He had withstood eons of temptation without a second thought.

Why her?

Why now?

Eoghan nearly called for Cael. If anyone could help him clear his head, it was Cael. But he hesitated when he thought about his friend being in the midst of fighting Bran. And knowing Cael, he would come in case Eoghan was in trouble.

He opened his eyes and looked at the thick, wooden door that separated him from Thea. No sounds had come from her room since she disappeared into it after they returned.

She had played the violin for about an hour but went silent thirty minutes ago. Leaving him to think of all the things he wanted to do to her.

"Thea," he whispered.

Only a handful of seconds passed before the door opened. He gazed into her beautiful brown eyes and tumbled head over heels for her. Eoghan couldn't fight it any longer.

He wrapped an arm around her, claiming her lips as he stepped into the room. With his other hand, he slammed the door shut as he continued to back her inside.

Her arms went around his neck, holding on tightly as she returned his kiss with fervor. She was once more wearing the sheep pajamas.

Suddenly, she pulled back and looked at him, her chest heaving. He smoothed her hair back from her face and took in her wondrous beauty.

"If you're going to kiss me and leave again, I'd rather you just leave now," she said.

Eoghan winced at the damage he'd inadvertently done. But he would make it up to her.

"I'm not walking away this time," he assured her.

"Then stop staring and kiss me."

He smiled as he leaned down to take her lips again. He splayed his hands across her back, pressing her against him as his blood rushed straight to his cock.

Elation swept through him at the sensation of holding her once more. He deepened the kiss as he tangled a hand in her blue tresses. Having her in his arms, kissing her, and letting the desire have its way was electrifying.

With the sweet, exotic taste of her filling his senses, he couldn't remember why he'd ever tried to keep her at arm's length.

He kissed down her neck and listened to her harsh breaths. She bent backward over his arm, her nails digging into his back when his mouth neared her breasts.

Everything she did, every sound she made was stirring, rousing. Evocative.

She yanked at his shirt, trying to take it off. With a thought, Eoghan removed it. She groaned as she ran her hands over his bare chest and lifted her head to look at him.

He paused in kissing across her chest to watch her expressions. When she pushed against him, he straightened, but he didn't release her.

"I have no words," she whispered. "You're perfection."

"I'm far from that."

She shook her head as her hand ran down his chest to his abdomen. "Not in my eyes. All I see is flawless magnificence." A frown formed when she reached the waist of his pants.

Her eyes snapped to his, and she raised a brow. So, she wanted him naked. Good, because that's exactly how he wanted her.

His eyes slid closed when she leaned forward and pressed her lips to the center of his chest. Then she moved to the left and placed soft, wet kisses over his heart before moving to the other side. She left a trail of heat in her wake while her hands caressed from his arms and shoulders to his stomach and back.

He clung to her as desire raged. He was unsure of the coming storm, but he knew he wanted to be in it with her. Only her.

She drove him wild while easing a part of him he hadn't known sought such relief. She pushed him, urging him to take chances, to let go and just . . . feel.

In all the years of his life, in all the places he'd seen and the people he'd encountered, not a single one of them could ever compare to the beauty and grace that was Thea.

Her lips reached his neck before kissing his chin and then his mouth. Right before he was about to claim her lips again, she put a finger over his mouth.

"I want to see you. Every glorious inch."

He immediately removed the rest of his clothes.

CHAPTER

seventeen

Thea had never beheld such brilliance before. Eoghan was spectacular in every way. His muscles were defined, the strength of his body evident not just in the thick sinew that covered his entire body but also in the way he held himself.

She couldn't catch her breath, couldn't hear anything but the sound of her blood pounding in her ears. After a couple of rough starts and abrupt halts, it looked as if Eoghan were ready to plunge into the fast-moving desire that had taken her instantly.

And it was about damn time that he jumped in with her.

With her hands flat on his chest, she couldn't decide what to kiss, touch, and lick first. Because she was going to taste every inch of him.

All her life, she'd been so ho-hum about guys and sex. But with Eoghan, it was like a switch had been flipped. She felt everything, ramped up on the highest setting. It was exhilarating and mind-blowing. And a little frightening, as well.

Just as her gaze dropped past his trim hips to his impressive cock, she heard a low moan pass his lips. No sooner did she recognize the sound than she found herself biting her lip as pleasure sucked her under in waves of ecstasy.

"Tá tú go hálainn."

She didn't know what he said, and it didn't matter. His husky voice, the way his gaze raked over her with possessiveness and yearning conveyed his meaning while his hands cupped her breasts.

He teased her nipples mercilessly. With each moan that fell from her lips, he doubled his efforts. Her breasts swelled—and her body ached.

Her knees threatened to buckle when he bent her back over his arm, and his hot mouth wrapped around a turgid peak. She cried out when he suckled, the pull going straight to her sex that hungered to feel him inside her.

Eoghan was ruthless in learning her body. She was deliriously helpless—and it felt amazing. While his lips did tantalizing things to her nipples, his free hand roamed her body in slow, methodical caresses as if he were putting her to memory.

She clung to him, shaking from the pleasure that filled her— yearning for more.

One minute, she was standing up, and the next, she was on the bed with Eoghan's glorious weight atop her. His mouth moved between her breasts as he placed hot kisses down her stomach. She lifted her head and watched him as he grew closer and closer to the juncture of her thighs.

His thick curtain of midnight hair fell to one side, sliding over her leg sensuously. His molten silver eyes briefly looked at her as his mouth hovered over her sex. His lips curved into a wicked smile before he lowered his head.

Her eyes rolled back in her head when she felt his warm breath an instant before his tongue touched her. She clutched the bed covers, her back arching at the exquisite pleasure that swirled through her and around her.

He relentlessly licked and laved her sex until she shook with the desire that longed to consume her. But he kept her on the edge, never letting her tip over the side.

She rocked her hips, seeking more. And he answered by slipping a finger inside her. Thea gasped and bucked her hips when he added a second digit and began to slowly move his hand in and out of her.

The orgasm was right there within reach, so close she could almost touch it. But it was almost as if Eoghan could read her thoughts, and each time she was about to climax, he pulled back.

It was a deliciously erotic torture. Each time, her desire built quicker, more intense. And each time she was denied, she sought the release even more.

And he wasn't even inside her yet.

Astounding. Incredible. Breathtaking.

Thea was all those things and more. Now that Eoghan knew the feel of her silky skin and her soft curves, there was no going back. Ever.

He was going to make her his, and he would accept whatever consequences came.

The taste of her desire filled his mouth and made his cock jump in expectation of thrusting deep inside her. He pushed his fingers within her tight sheath and groaned at the way her body clamped around him.

She stiffened, a signal that she was about to peak. He stopped moving his tongue and hand to let the desire ease its hold. He glanced up at her. The sight of her flushed skin, her parted lips, and her head rolling from side to side as she gripped the bedding made him hunger for her even more.

She was beautiful, but in the throes of passion, she was glorious. Stunning.

Absolutely resplendent.

With her writhing in rapture, he couldn't believe he had ever had the strength to pull away from her. He could spend eternity bringing her pleasure, and it would still never be enough for him.

Her hips rock against his hand, seeking friction. Her sex and clit were swollen and wet with need. He gazed down at her entrance where his fingers were, and his balls tightened when he imagined guiding his cock there.

He lifted his gaze to Thea's face and saw her staring at him. He slid his fingers inside her slowly as he thumbed her clit.

Her eyes widened as her chest heaved. He held her gaze and continued to pleasure her with slow thrusts of his fingers while increasing the speed of his thumb.

"Tá tú go hálainn, you are gorgeous," he murmured.

After the many times he'd brought her to the edge before backing off, it didn't take her any time before her body tightened. But this time, he didn't draw back.

This time, he pushed her over the pinnacle and right into her orgasm.

He rose up on his knees and palmed his cock when she cried out, her back arching off the bed while her body convulsed as she peaked.

Eoghan ran his hand up and down his length, fighting the

need to remove his fingers and bury himself inside her. It was a torturous wait for her to come down from her climax.

With her body still spasming around his fingers, he removed them and positioned himself between her legs. With his cock at her entrance, he paused and met her gaze. She looked at him through slitted eyes.

"Yes," she whispered breathlessly.

Eoghan placed his hands on either side of her head and slowly pushed into her tight, wet heat. She felt so good. He looked down at her as she gripped his waist.

He groaned when she bit her lip once he was fully seated. Her bright eyes stared up at him. Then, she wrapped her legs around his waist and locked her ankles together.

It was the way she caressed his face that made his heart trip over itself. Thea wasn't just any Halfling. He'd recognized it from the beginning, but he hadn't wanted to admit it. Now, he didn't have a choice.

Thea sighed when Eoghan began to thrust deeply and slowly. The feeling of him sliding in and out of her was exquisite, just as she had known it would be.

It wasn't long until his rhythm increased. She could do nothing but lay there as he played her with expert precision. He knew just how to move his body to give her the most pleasure.

She drifted into a place that was nothing but ecstasy and bliss. Somewhere where no one existed by the two of them.

To her surprise, she felt the now familiar desire tighten low in her belly once more. She met his thrusts, eager to feel the wash of pleasure again.

She hurtled over the precipice into a void of rapture that slid sensuously along her body. It wrapped tightly around her, cocooning her in pleasure until her limbs were weighed down and she could barely open her eyes.

Eoghan then pulled out of her and flipped her onto her stomach before grabbing her ankles and pulling her toward the edge of the bed until her legs hung off.

Then he filled her with one hard thrust. She moaned as he entered her. God, he felt so damn good. How had she ever been disinterested in sex? Then again, none of her lovers had been Eoghan.

His fingers dug into her hips as he plunged into her again and again. She once more slipped into that space between worlds and simply let herself experience every wonderful second.

He fell over her, his thrusts growing short and fast until he buried himself deep and stilled. She felt his seed feel her, and while she realized they hadn't used protection, she wasn't worried. Because the idea of making a child with Eoghan excited her.

After several long moments, he moved aside her hair and kissed her cheek before pulling out of her. He then lifted her in his arms and climbed into bed.

She snuggled against him as he pulled the covers over them. It was impossible to keep her eyes open after being pleasured so thoroughly.

There was a smile on her face as well. She couldn't remember the last time she had been so happy. It was a moment to be treasured and looked back on years from now.

"I'll never push you away again," Eoghan whispered before kissing her brow.

"Tell me we'll do this again?" she asked.

He chuckled. "Definitely. I couldn't stay away from you if my life depended upon it."

She smiled and kissed his chest as sleep pulled at her.

Aisling put her ear to Thea's door and listened. She grinned when she picked up both Eoghan's and Thea's voices. It was about bloody time.

She turned around and found Cathal sitting on one of the chairs in the rotunda while sharpening his sword. He hadn't been there when she arrived, and she hated how he kept sneaking up on her.

"Eavesdropping?" he drawled, keeping his gaze on his weapon.

She shrugged and walked to him. "I wondered if Eoghan finally pulled his head out of his arse and realized what was before him."

"For someone who rags about men all the time, you sure are a romantic."

She was going to have to be more careful to hide not just the pain of her past, but her secrets, as well. "What's it to you?"

"I just want to know if you're going to try and kick my ass for being a man or not."

She raised a brow as she crossed her arms over her chest. "You're safe. Unless you treat a woman wrong. Then I'll be coming for you."

He turned dark red eyes to her. "I'd expect nothing less."

She gave him a nod and dropped her arms as she turned on her heel. She only got two steps before Cathal's deep voice reached her.

"Whoever hurt you was a fool. I hope you castrated him. And, for what it's worth, there's nothing wrong with being romantic."

She paused and let his words sink in. Without turning around, she said, "Thank you."

Aisling continued toward her chamber, wondering how many more times Cathal would surprise her.

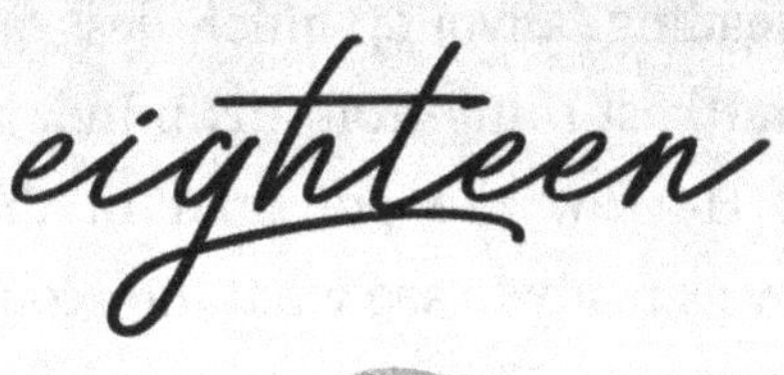

CHAPTER eighteen

Everything had changed. Eoghan couldn't deny that fact. After the other realm, he'd told himself that he would get out and find his way back to his brothers and that everything would go back to the way it was—after killing Bran, of course.

But that had been a lie he'd told himself. Something that had gotten him through the ordeal. Even if Erith hadn't given him leadership of the new Reapers, he was too changed by his ordeal for things to go back to normal.

Then there was Thea. Being with her forced him to see how things really were. And he discovered that he quite liked it. A surprising occurrence, to be sure.

He held Thea tighter. In all his long eons, he'd never once believed that he would ever again hold another in his arms. He'd been just fine with that, too.

In fact, he reconciled himself to accept a great many things. All while he'd been weighed down by the past. He could clearly recall how holding onto the horrible events shaped him—how he had allowed the past to influence him.

The idea of leading anyone, much less another group of Reapers, was the farthest thing from his mind. Now, however, he relished the role. He saw the potential in the Fae under his command, and he was ready to see what they could do.

Eoghan remained with Thea for another hour, listening to her breathing, feeling her body alongside his. Then he kissed her forehead and gently extracted himself from her limbs to check in with the others.

He strode across the room as he called his clothes to him. By the time he opened the door, he was fully dressed. Eoghan quietly shut it behind him and made his way to the center room.

Rordan was flipping one of his many knives in the air. He caught the blade and grinned. "All I'll say is that it's about time. The sexual tension between the two of you was difficult to miss."

"I know I said I was keeping to my vows," Eoghan began.

Rordan held up a hand to stop him. "Take whatever happiness you can when you find it."

"Wise words."

Rordan shrugged and glanced at the ground. "My mother was a wise woman."

"She passed it on to you."

He sheathed the knife at his hip as he stood. "I may not have told you, but I'm glad you're the one leading us."

"That means a lot. Thank you."

"You know our pasts, don't you?"

Eoghan nodded slowly.

Rordan let out a sigh. "That's what I thought."

"I may know what happened, but I'm not judging you on it."

"You should," he replied.

Eoghan frowned. "You've proven who you really are. Otherwise, Erith never would have chosen you to be a Reaper."

"I'm the Fae I am now because she saw something in me that I never saw in myself."

"Whatever the reason, I'm glad you're with us."

Rordan bowed his head. "I waited for you because I had an idea."

"About?" Eoghan pressed.

"The Seeker. When we found him, he looked like he was after something."

"You mean he was on another job?"

"Maybe," Rordan said with a shrug of his shoulders. "Or he wanted something."

Eoghan clenched his fists as it dawned on him. "He knows us. Specifically me. There is one who would give anything to know where I am."

"Bran," Rordan said. "Do you really believe the Seeker was trying to find him?"

"We know Bran has been taking Dark. "

Rordan jerked his chin to Thea's door. "Shall I guard her?"

Eoghan wanted to be the one to take down Bran, but he also knew that wouldn't be today. And there were things he needed to tell Thea. "Take two of the others and see if you can find Bran. No doubt our Seeker will be there. Call to me when you find them."

Rordan nodded and vanished to carry out Eoghan's orders. Eoghan then teleported into Thea's room. He wanted to let her sleep, but there was no telling when Rordan might return—or when Eoghan would have to leave.

He sat on the edge of the bed and lifted one of the pale blue locks of her hair to twirl around his finger. After he'd let the strand fall from his fingers, he stroked her face.

Thea's forehead furrowed as she rolled away from him with a grunt. He smiled and leaned over to brush his lips against her ear.

"Five more minutes," she murmured.

"I'd give it to you if I had it."

She rolled onto her back and opened her eyes. She yawned sleepily. "What is it?"

Eoghan started to tell her about the news about Bran, but then he realized she knew nothing of him. In fact, Eoghan hadn't told her anything about himself.

"You're frowning," Thea said as she tucked the covers under her arms and pushed up so that her shoulders rested against the headboard. "I don't like when you do that."

"I told you I was once commander of the Fae army. What I didn't tell you was that I had a family. A wife and a beautiful son."

Thea put her hand on his arm. "You don't have to do this. I can see how painful it is."

"I will carry the pain of losing my child for eternity, but more than that, I want you to know."

"Good."

He drew in a deep breath. "As an orphan, I craved family. I dreamed of being a father. I wanted dozens of children. I wanted the noise and chaos and clutter. I didn't care if the woman I loved was lowborn or not. You see, in Fae culture, we're still divided into nobility, royalty, and commoners."

"You were a commoner."

"I was, but I didn't care. I worked hard because I had ambition. My fighting skills came naturally, so I joined the army. It wasn't long before I moved up the ranks, not because of my skills, but because I was driven to succeed. And the higher my rank, the more I was in contact with the nobility."

Thea nodded. "That sounds about right."

"It was during one of the balls that I first saw Tiann. She was beautiful, yes, but out of my league. I knew it and didn't try to pursue her."

"I'm guessing she didn't feel the same?"

Eoghan shook his head. "Like so many women, she kept apprised of who garnered new rank and how quickly. Apparently, she had been following my career. When I didn't go to her, she came to me. We danced the entire night and were together every chance we got after that. Six months later, we were married. And a year later, she was pregnant with our first child."

"Sounds like a happy ending."

"It should've been." He leaned his head back on the headboard. "I learned by chance that she had been preventing herself from getting with child and that she became pregnant by accident. If I hadn't discovered she was carrying my son, I think she might have gotten rid of him."

Thea wrinkled her nose. "I'm not liking her at all."

He smiled at her candor. "She didn't have an easy pregnancy. Her family wasn't too happy about our marriage, but they accepted it. They helped Tiann while I was away. I made it back in time to see my son born. He was the most precious thing I'd ever held."

"What did you name him?"

"Eachann."

"I like it," Thea said.

Eoghan turned his head to her and smiled. "He was the light of my life. He always had a smile on his face. Such a happy baby. But while I was delighted with him, Tiann was not. She didn't enjoy that Eachann took up the time she used to spend with her friends, and she began leaving him with her parents."

"You didn't like that, did you?"

"No." Eoghan remembered the anger that had swept through him when he discovered what Tiann had been doing. "I'd already missed the first two years of my son's life being called away on missions, so I decided to withdraw from the army and raise my child. I believed it was the perfect solution, but Tiann didn't see it that way. In her eyes, without my rank, I was just another commoner, and she couldn't stand that."

Thea's eyes widened in surprise. "I've known bitches like that."

"I refused to let her dissuade me from my decision. We argued an entire evening about it, and I went to bed. I don't know what woke me. Maybe the silence. I went to check on Eachann and found blood everywhere. I picked up his lifeless body and saw Tiann walk from a corner. Her eyes were red now that she had murdered our son. She smiled at me before teleporting behind me and shoving the blade into my back."

Thea shifted to face him and put her hand atop his. "You died with your son in your arms."

"Losing him was so great that it consumed me."

"And why you took a vow of silence."

He nodded. "I've never told another that story."

"What was done to you is so horrible that I have no words."

He lifted her hand and entwined his fingers with hers. "It's enough that you listened."

"There's more you want to tell me, isn't there?"

Eoghan briefly looked away. "There's Bran."

"Ah. Bran," she said with a twist of her lips. "I've heard you and the others say his name."

"He was one of the first seven Reapers. He fell in love with a Light Fae and told her what he was."

Thea's face creased as she winced. "And Death killed her because of the rule."

"Yes. Bran went crazy and divided the other six of us. He and the ones who followed him killed our leader, while Cael and I battled them. We slew the other three, leaving just Cael, Bran, and myself. Cael managed to get the upper hand, but before he could kill Bran, Death arrived and tossed Bran into a prison world she'd created just for him."

"I would say good, but I gather he got out."

"He did, and he's trying to kill Death and us. I believe the Seeker intends to tell Bran that I've returned."

Thea sat up. "What can we do to prevent that?"

"Nothing until Rordan finds Bran and the Seeker."

Thea gaped at him. "Why aren't you looking? Tell me you didn't stay behind because you feared I'd get pissed that you weren't here when I woke."

"That might have been one of the reasons," he replied.

Thea let the covers drop as she moved to her knees and cupped his face with her hands. "You know Bran better than the others. You and Cael. Go to your friend. Together, you will find Bran and stop the Seeker."

"And then make the Seeker give us the answers about you that he evaded the last time."

She waved away his words. "Yes, I want to know, but that can wait. I can't imagine what will happen if Bran kills all of you and Death."

"He's taking Death's magic and power already. If he kills her, he'll take her place."

"Then you must stop him."

He gazed into her brown eyes in wonderment. With her by his side, he believed he could do anything. "I won't leave you unguarded."

"I'll be fine. Go."

He glanced down at her naked body, remembering their lovemaking. "I'll be back as quick as I can."

"And I'll be waiting," she promised with a smile.

Eoghan pulled her close for a kiss before he stood and went to find Cael.

nineteen

Knowing the power and authority Eoghan held made Thea all tingly inside. She hugged her knees to her chest and smiled. She didn't have a doubt in her mind that Eoghan would find Bran.

It was the Seeker that caused her worry.

There was something unsettling about him. He'd been kind—well, as nice as a kidnapper could be. But he'd still taken her. On whose orders, was the real question.

Thea recalled the feeling of someone being in the cottage with her. The presence hadn't felt exactly threatening, but she hadn't gotten that warm, fuzzy feeling either.

For all the questions plaguing her, she knew that, somehow, Eoghan would sort it all out—despite having worries of his own.

Thea turned her head to the pillows. There was no way she could sleep now with her mind filled with so many thoughts and concerns about Eoghan and the Reapers.

She threw off the covers and rose from the bed to dress. After running her fingers through her hair, she swept it up into a messy bun and walked from her room.

Only to come to a halt at the sight of a woman lounging in one of the chairs with one long leg crossed over the other. The woman's swirling silver eyes were piercing and deadly.

With one look, Thea knew that whoever the woman was, she was a major player, someone with not only power but also clout.

And someone not to be taken lightly.

Thea didn't need to ask if the woman was Fae. The designation dripped from every inch of her—as did a regal flare that only someone who lived the life could pull off.

The woman uncrossed her legs and stood. She wore all white from the white-on-white-striped shirt that dipped low enough to show ample cleavage to the pants that skimmed her legs to the slinky stilettos.

"I'm not a fan of the blue hair," the woman stated. Her condemning gaze raked up and down Thea's black attire. "Or the clothes."

"I don't care. I dress to please myself."

"That's shite," she replied and then waved her hand.

The next thing Thea knew, her hair was down and she was in a short, yellow dress with black over-the-knee stiletto boots. She lifted a lock of hair that hung over her shoulder and spotted the light brown tresses that she hadn't seen in years.

She glared at the woman. "I don't give a damn who you are, you had no right to do that."

"I have every right."

Thea opened her mouth to reply, but the woman strode to her and grabbed her wrist before teleporting them away.

While Eoghan knew calling to Cael in order to find Bran was the right thing to do, he couldn't shake the feeling that he should have left someone with Thea.

The wards and spells he and his Reapers had put up were strong enough to keep others out—well, all but the most powerful Fae like Death.

"I know that look."

Eoghan's gaze snapped up to find Cael standing before him. "Thank you for coming."

"Tell me what's wrong?"

"Nothing," Eoghan said with a shake of his head.

Cael lifted a brow and waited.

Eoghan let out a long sigh. "I have a feeling I shouldn't have left Thea."

"Thea?" Cael asked with raised brows.

Eoghan ran a hand over his face and quickly filled Cael in on how Thea had saved him. With every word, he wanted to return to her or send one of the others to check on her.

"Any particular reason you have that feeling?" Cael asked.

Eoghan looked at Edinburgh Castle to his left before glancing down the cliff below. "She was taken by a Fae a few days ago. I only found her because he allowed it."

"Who is this Fae?"

"I don't know. Rordan calls him the Seeker because, apparently, he can get anything you want. He also works for both the Light and the Dark."

Cael nodded slowly. "So, he's someone who knows his way around."

"Aye. He also knows who I am. By name."

"Dammit," Cael mumbled.

"My Reapers and I tracked him to the Dark Palace and tried to find out who wanted him to kidnap Thea, but he wouldn't tell us."

"But you figured out what he's up to."

Eoghan shrugged. "It's a hunch, but I kept coming back to how he knew my name and that I was a Reaper. I don't think he's working with Bran. Yet."

"You think he's going to use the information about you to get in with Bran."

"I do," Eoghan said. "Whoever wanted Thea is powerful, and the Seeker is afraid of them."

Cael crossed his arms over his chest. "Why not go to Balladyn or Usaeil then? Why Bran?"

"Because he either doesn't or can't trust Balladyn or Usaeil. Which leads me back to Bran. My team is searching for Bran, but I realized that you might know where he is."

Cael smiled. "That I do. The last mission we had was in Killarney."

"With the black sword," Eoghan said, recalling the story.

"Bran is obsessed with getting the weapon. He's been at the property ever since."

Impatience pushed Eoghan. "Take me there."

Without another word, Cael touched Eoghan's arm and brought them to Ettie O'Byrne's property. Both were veiled before they arrived. And just as Cael said, Bran was there with his men, tearing up the land in search of the sword.

Eoghan sent out a call to his Reapers. Within minutes, all six of them arrived. His team looked at Cael with awe as he greeted each of them.

It was then that Eoghan felt his old friend's gaze on him. When he looked over, Cael was grinning.

"You've changed," Cael said.

Eoghan gave a shake of his head while trying to hide his grin. "If the Seeker is here, which I know he is, he'll be veiled until he can get close to Bran."

"What are we waiting for then?" Dubhan asked.

Cathal smiled in anticipation and pulled his sword from the scabbard at his back. "No matter what, the Seeker isn't getting away this time."

Eoghan nodded to them. "Fan out, but don't get close to Bran. It's not our time for him yet."

"But soon," Aisling said before teleporting away.

When Eoghan's Reapers had spread out, Cael turned to him. "You have a good team."

"I do."

"And you've accepted your role, I see."

Eoghan felt his lips curve when he thought of Thea and how she had opened his eyes to a great many things. "I have."

"I'm happy for you."

"I'll be happy when I find out who's after Thea and why."

Cael's head swung in Bran's direction. "You really don't believe it's Bran?"

"He would've had her killed. The person who wants Thea has other plans. The Seeker didn't harm a hair on her head."

"There are powerful Fae, both Dark and Light."

"Aye, but the Seeker is one who could get away from a Reaper while we were questioning him. That means whoever he works for has to be of considerable power."

Cael's brows snapped together. "Shite."

"Exactly."

"The list narrows considerably."

Eoghan nodded as he flattened his lips. "I know."

"Who is Thea? What makes her so important?"

"I don't know. She's a Halfling orphan without knowledge of either of her parents. Her only ability is her music, but it is a considerable one."

"It has to be in order for it to have pulled you from that other realm," Cael said.

Eoghan swung his gaze to Bran. For so many months he'd been consumed with finding the ex-Reaper, but now, all Eoghan wanted to do was locate the Seeker and get the information they needed.

Yet, Bran was a reminder of his old life and the betrayal that had made Cael leader. All because Bran had fallen in love and shared their secret.

"How long have you been in love with Thea?" Cael asked.

Eoghan's gaze snapped to him. "What gave it away?"

"You look at Bran with understanding now."

Eoghan rubbed the back of his neck. "I tried not to feel anything for her. I wanted to keep to the vow I made to Erith when I became a Reaper."

"But the heart won out."

"It did, and once I gave in, the feeling was incredible."

Cael looked away.

Eoghan studied his old friend's profile. "How does it feel to be surrounded by couples in your group?"

"At times, lonely." Cael slid his gaze back to Eoghan. "If I'm being honest. But I'll only admit that to you."

"You do know there's a good chance we'll lose this battle with Bran."

"I know," Cael said after a brief hesitation.

Eoghan held Cael's gaze. "Then perhaps you should tell Erith your feelings."

"I don't know what you're talking about."

"Don't bother denying it. I've seen you for too many centuries staring off into space thinking of someone. For a long time, I thought it was a woman from before you were a Reaper, , But I've seen the way you look at Erith. Oh, you hide it well," Eoghan said when concern flashed over Cael's face. "But I've known you far longer than the others."

Cael swallowed and was silent for a long time. "I've done a great many foolish things in my life, and I'll not add going to her to tell her whatever it is that I might be feeling."

"So you'll love her from afar?"

"It's for the best."

Eoghan was about to disagree when Bradach called his name. Immediately, Eoghan and Cael went to the Reaper, who, along with Torin, held the Seeker between them.

"You're making a mistake," the Fae said between clenched teeth.

Eoghan and Cael looked at each other before they smiled and took the Seeker to a vast field far from Bran. Eoghan and Cael stood before the Fae while Eoghan's team surrounded them.

"Tell me your name," Eoghan demanded.

The Fae lifted a brow. "Why?"

"Because it'll save us a trip to speak to Death," Cael said. "Death's gaze isn't turned to you currently, and trust me when I say you want to keep it that way."

"Xaneth," the Fae finally relented.

Eoghan gave a nod of appreciation. "Now, it's time you tell me exactly who is after Thea and why."

Xaneth looked from Cael to Eoghan. "How much power do you have as a Reaper?"

"Why?" Cael demanded.

"I'm wondering if you could win a fight say with the King of the Dark," Xaneth replied with a shrug.

Eoghan hid his frown. "How do you know we're Reapers?"

"It's amazing what you can pick up when you listen."

"No one knows us," Cael stated.

Xaneth lifted a brow and twisted his lips. "I'll admit, you are all very careful, but I followed Talin at the Light castle and learned a lot."

Eoghan exchanged a look with Cael before he faced Xaneth. "In other words, you pieced it all together. You don't really know what a Reaper does?"

"My livelihood is made on gathering information I can use later and acquiring things others can't get. I've learned to make my way in the Light, Dark, and mortal worlds. I listen, and I watch. Whispers of Reapers began not long after Talin arrived at the Light Castle," Xaneth explained.

Eoghan was fast losing patience. "I don't care how you found out. No Fae who knows our secret lives long. So I suggest you tell me who is after Thea?"

Xaneth narrowed his gaze on Eoghan. "I'll tell you if you keep me alive."

"We can't promise that," Cael said.

Xaneth shrugged. "It's definitely someone you'd be interested in knowing."

"Fine," Eoghan said. "I'll make a case for you to Death if the name you give us warrants such attention."

Xaneth smiled as he said, "Thea is Usaeil's daughter."

CHAPTER
twenty

"Get your damn hands off me," Thea stated as she jerked away from the woman—Fae—who was clearly mad as a box of frogs.

Silver eyes flashed with fury. "No one talks to me that way and lives."

"Then I'm going to make this really easy for you," Thea declared. "I know you're Fae, but that doesn't scare me. I'm tired of your kind believing you have the right to take me whenever and wherever you please. In fact, I'm fekking pissed right now. So, return me. Immediately."

"No."

It wasn't as if Thea actually thought the Fae would do as she commanded, but she was teetering on the verge of a meltdown, and she refused to crumble in front of this woman.

Worse was the fact that Thea wasn't sure what to think of the Reapers anymore. Eoghan had assured her that she'd be safe beneath the cathedral, that no one could get past their wards and spells. And yet, a Fae had.

The woman smiled and tossed back her long, lustrous, black hair. "You don't know who I am?"

"No," Thea said and crossed her arms over her chest while shooting the Fae her best I-don't-give-a-shite look.

"Most mortals recognize me for my work."

"Good for you."

The anger was back in an instant. "If you knew who I was, you wouldn't be so cavalier with your attitude."

"Obviously, you want me to be scared, impressed, or awed by you. I can't figure out if it's this mortal image I should fear or the Fae one. Just tell me your name so I can give the appropriate look and we can move on."

"I forgot about you for many years."

Thea was shocked by the comment. And quite frankly, unsure how to respond. "Okay."

They stared at each other for a long moment before Thea looked around the room. She didn't want to be captivated by the lavish white and gold surroundings. But she was.

The ceilings appeared to be over thirty feet high with a design painted in gold that she couldn't quite make out. The room was large, but not overly decorated. In fact, some might consider it sparse.

When she returned her gaze to the Fae, Thea asked, "Where are we?"

"My home."

"Which is?" she prompted.

The Fae grinned. "The Light Castle."

Thea swallowed, her arms dropping to her sides. She forced

herself to remain still instead of backing up a few steps as she longed to do. "And you are?"

"Usaeil, the Queen of the Light."

The room began to spin, and Thea's knees went weak. This couldn't be happening. "I'm not in the mood for jokes."

"And I'm not joking."

Thea studied Usaeil. "What do you want with me?"

"I'm not sure," she replied with a small frown.

Of all the things Thea had thought the queen might say, that wasn't one of them. She kept thinking of the Red Queen in Alice in Wonderland shouting, "Off with her head!"

Usaeil walked past her. Thea turned and watched the queen move to a set of impossibly tall, arched windows. Then Usaeil said, "There is very little that anyone knows about me—mortal or Fae. I've made sure of that."

"Are you scared of others knowing you?" Thea wasn't sure why she asked.

Usaeil glanced at her over her shoulder. "I've been in power for untold eons. Everyone always wants something from me. For a long while, I forgot who I was. Then I found something I wanted, someone that I craved with every part of my soul. But he was with another."

"Yeah. That always sucks, but it happens. Even to queens." Thea couldn't hold back the eye roll.

"Not to me," came the terse reply.

Thea frowned as she studied Usaeil. "What did you do?"

"I made sure he was free. It actually took little effort. He didn't know I instigated it. As powerful as the Dragon King was, he missed my interference. To this day, he still doesn't know my part in it. And he never will."

Thea knew she was hearing a secret that had never been shared before. She wasn't stupid. No one imparted such confidences without ensuring they would never be repeated. And the queen was just the type to order Thea's death so the secret would remain hidden.

"So, I suppose you and this Dragon King are together now?" Thea asked. Despite knowing that she would never leave the castle alive, she still wanted to hear the rest of the story.

"No," Usaeil answered.

Thea almost grinned at the answer. She didn't care how powerful a person was, no one had the right to destroy a relationship simply because they wanted someone who was already taken. "And the woman who was with him before?"

Usaeil whirled around, her eyes filled with such hatred that it caused Thea to step back. "I tried to get rid of Rhi. I guided her into a realm that would ensure she never returned, but once again, I was thwarted, and Rhi was saved."

Inwardly, Thea did a little fist pump. Especially if this were the same Rhi Eoghan had spoken of. Thea didn't know Rhi or the Dragon King, but it made her happy they were both still alive, and that Usaeil hadn't gotten what she wanted.

Usaeil raised a perfectly arched black brow. "My misery pleases you?"

"We don't always get what we want. Even you. Magic or not, power or not, you had no right to break up Rhi and her man. You deserve what you got."

The queen chuckled, the sound sinister and creepy. "I'm sure there are those who would agree with you, but I didn't get this position without seizing what I want. I'll eventually get everything I covet. I always do. I've got my sights set on the King of Dragon Kings. And Constantine will be mine."

"Regardless of what he wants?" Thea queried.

"He wants me. Con just doesn't know it yet."

"The words of someone who has never been denied anything."

Usaeil grinned. "I worried you might be weak after being raised by mortals. It seems I was wrong. Others tremble before me, but you attempt to put me in my place."

Unease snaked down Thea's spine. "That pleases you. Why?"

"I would expect nothing less from my daughter."

The words registered, but Thea refused to believe them. Her mind screamed in refusal, but she calmly replied, "No."

"Do you have any idea how many would love to be in your place?" Usaeil asked angrily as she stalked to her.

Thea didn't back down. She stood her ground and retorted, "Did it ever enter your mind that I didn't want to know you? I couldn't care less if you are a queen or living on the streets. You gave me up. I want nothing to do with you."

"Twenty-eight years ago, your life was in my hands. It is once again."

Thea shook her head as she laughed. The threat hung between them, real and tangible. "Am I supposed to be glad you didn't kill me when I was born?"

"I never let any of the others survive. Most, I ended still in my womb."

"And my father?"

Usaeil shrugged uncaringly. "Some mortal who struck my fancy for the night."

The woman before her sickened Thea. Worse, Usaeil was her mother. The same blood flowed through both of them. Every time Thea thought of trying to find her mom, something had told her to let it go. Now, she knew why.

"You shouldn't be in power. The Light are supposed to be all that is good and pure," Thea said.

Usaeil barked in laughter. "Who told you that? Xaneth?"

"I don't know who that is."

"He's the one I hired to kidnap you. He's also the one who took you from the cottage and attempted to hide you below the church. But I can find you anywhere."

That angered Thea, but she also noted that Usaeil, as powerful as she thought herself, knew nothing of the Reapers. "If you could find me, then why did you need Xaneth to kidnap me?"

"I wasn't sure if I wanted to kill you or talk to you."

"And you needed someone to snatch me off the streets to figure that out?"

Usaeil shrugged. "I wanted you to myself."

"You're off your rocker."

"I'll find Xaneth and punish him for his deception. I never intended to allow him to live anyway, but now, he'll die slowly."

Thea made a sound in the back of her throat in disdain. "Because he disobeyed you?"

"Because he's my nephew."

That's when it hit Thea. She was standing before a monster with a beautiful face, but still a monster. "You killed your family, didn't you?"

Usaeil gave her a flat look. "I took the throne from my grandfather. It was so easy. He never saw it coming. I originally banished the rest of my family, but I soon came to realize they posed a threat to me. And my throne. So, I had them hunted down and killed."

"You've murdered your family and your own children. Yet you say you want this King of Dragon Kings. How do you expect that to work? And if you become pregnant again, will you kill that offspring, too?"

Usaeil's face went slack with shock. "Never. And it will work with Con because he's a King."

"You've erased anyone who has a claim to the throne. Why bring me here and tell me all of this? I would never have known my heritage, and I would've been much happier that way."

The queen closed the distance between them and reached out. Thea dodged her hand, uncaring if it pissed Usaeil off or not. Thea didn't want the queen touching her again. Ever.

Usaeil's lips thinned with her fury. "You're making it so easy for me to kill you."

"Then do it. Because I won't change. I won't beg you for my life. I won't tell you that you're right about everything. I won't worship you. What I'll do is tell you that you're daft and should be committed. I'll tell you that every Fae should know of your actions and decide your punishment. I'll tell you that the last thing you should be is Queen of the Light."

Thea drew in a breath to continue, but she found herself roughly slammed back against a wall. Though Usaeil was across the room, Thea felt a hand around her throat, slowly squeezing.

She gasped for air, her feet dangling above the floor and banging against the wall as she fought to get a foothold of some kind. But she knew it was pointless.

From the moment Usaeil had admitted to killing her other children and debating what to do with Thea, she'd known she was going to die. She had nothing to battle a Fae queen with, so she didn't stand a chance.

She almost called out for Eoghan, but she hesitated. Thea wanted to see him again, to tell him that she had fallen madly, wildly in love with him, but that time had passed. She didn't want him to see her die, and she didn't know if he could take on Usaeil.

If it were the last thing she did, Thea would ensure that the queen knew nothing of the Reapers. Eoghan and his team would learn what became of her, and maybe then, Death would have to take a look at Usaeil and judge her.

Thea closed her eyes. She no longer wanted to look upon the face of her mother. Her mind took her to a place away from the pain where she was with Eoghan and her music.

Everything else fell away. Usaeil, the beautiful white and gold room, and most especially, the agony of being suffocated. Her musings took her to the safety of Eoghan's arms while music surrounded her like a warm blanket.

The melody was so loud that it came from every direction. Or maybe it was projecting in every direction from her.

With her lungs burning, she whispered Eoghan's name in her head and let the song within her grow louder until her ears rang with it.

And somewhere in the melody, she thought she heard Eoghan say her name. It made her smile.

Her life had never been easy, but she'd found contentment in music. It wasn't until she met Eoghan that she discovered passion and love and learned what true happiness was.

Most people never experienced such bliss, and while she'd only had a short time with Eoghan, it was enough.

Thea tried to pull in some air, but she heard a loud crack as her larynx was crushed. She clung to an image of Eoghan as her heart gave its final beat.

twenty-one

Panic mixed with alarm and knotted with the rising tide of rage. Eoghan digested the news Xaneth had spilled so cheerfully. Some might find the information heartening, because of Usaeil's power.

But Eoghan knew the truth.

"You've got to be fekking kidding?" Bradach murmured.

Rordan wrinkled his nose. "No one can help who their parents are."

"This is bad, especially for Thea," Aisling said.

Cathal snorted loudly. "You think?"

"We're Reapers," Dubhan stated. "We can go after Usaeil."

Torin rubbed his hands together. "I'm game."

"We can't," Cael said.

Rordan's gaze jerked to Cael. "Why the hell not?"

"What has she done?" Aisling asked. "Other than have Thea kidnapped. And we made sure no one could get to Thea."

"And Death hasn't judged Usaeil," Bradach pointed out.

Eoghan's mind was filled with everyone's words as well as his growing concern. As soon as he heard Xaneth's laughter, his gaze was on the Fae.

"Do you have something to add?" Eoghan demanded.

Xaneth looked around at all of them. "You wonder why I sought out Bran instead of you. You act like you have power, yet you can't do anything without Death's permission."

Torin walked until he stood nose-to-nose with Xaneth. "Oh, I can do something. Shall I show you?"

Xaneth shoved Torin back and looked at Eoghan. "You think Thea's safe? She's Usaeil's daughter. That means that, no matter where Thea is, the queen can find her."

"Then why did she send you after her?" Cael questioned.

Xaneth gave him a flat look. "Usaeil doesn't get her hands dirty with anything. Not even killing her own family."

Eoghan immediately teleported to the rooms beneath the cathedral. He shouted Thea's name and ran from chamber to chamber, but they were empty. Just as he'd suspected they would be.

He walked back to the rotunda to find his team along with Cael and Xaneth. When his gaze landed on the Seeker, Eoghan launched himself at the Fae and slammed him up against the wall.

"You put an innocent life on the line to save your own worthless hide," Eoghan stated, letting rage lace his words and show on his face. "I should end your miserable life this second."

"Do it," Xaneth goaded. "I'd rather die by your hand than Usaeil's. I've lived my entire life hiding from her. She killed off my family one by one until I was the only one left. I thought by helping her, she would allow me back into the Light."

Eoghan fisted his hand, wanting to do violence. "You say an awful lot without ever really stating anything."

"Usaeil is my aunt," Xaneth said after a hesitation. "She took the throne from her grandfather after convincing one of the King's Guard that he was turning Dark. The guard killed the King, and Usaeil took the throne."

Eoghan took a step back in shock as Cael walked up beside him. Eoghan gave a shake of his head. "That can't be correct. The Fae would've heard something."

Xaneth snorted loudly. "Where did Usaeil's family go? Her parents, brothers, sisters, and extended family?"

Eoghan shared a looked with Cael before sliding his gaze back to Xaneth. "You're saying Usaeil killed everyone?"

"She never laid a hand on any of us. In the dead of night, she threw us out of the castle and proclaimed herself queen. She told the Fae we were banished and never allowed to return. She convinced others to kill anyone of her blood for her, and then later, she put together a small group of Fae she dubbed Trackers to find and kill the rest of us. It wasn't that long ago that I left my little sister to find some food and carry out a job. I returned in time to see the Trackers kill her. She was only a child."

Torin's face twisted in anguish. "It takes a sick fek to kill a child."

"Aye," Cael murmured.

Eoghan shook his head, his gut churning with dread. "This is unfathomable."

"My other aunt, Usaeil's sister, warned me that she could never be trusted. Usaeil had no idea I was alive until I told her because I wanted to return to the Light and resume my place among them. I don't want the throne. I'm just tired of hiding," Xaneth said.

"She didn't kill Thea when she was born," Rordan pointed out.

A small kernel of hope sprang to life within Eoghan.

Xaneth rubbed the back of his neck as he glanced at the floor.

"In my time as Seeker, when I moved freely between the Light and Dark, I heard whispers of Usaeil destroying her babies while still in the womb."

"Now I'm going to be sick," Aisling said, her face ashen.

Xaneth dropped the glamour to reveal bright silver eyes and short, black hair. "This is who I really am."

Eoghan ran a hand down his face. "What does Usaeil want with Thea now?"

"She didn't share that with me," Xaneth replied. "But the queen leaves no blood relative alive who has a claim to the throne."

Eoghan immediately thought of the Warrior, Phelan. His head snapped to Cael.

"I was thinking the same thing. I just contacted Daire, and he's going to find Rhi," Cael said.

Now, Eoghan knew why Rhi went to such lengths to keep the Warrior's Fae blood a secret. "If Rhi knew any of this, she'd kill Usaeil herself."

"She doesn't know," Xaneth said.

Cathal crossed his arms over his chest. "How do you know that?"

"I might be banished, but I have connections in both the Light and Dark. There are those who say Usaeil is afraid of Rhi's power, which is why the queen befriended Rhi and kept her close," Xaneth explained.

Eoghan sliced his hand through the air. "As interesting as all of this is, I need to find Thea."

"Then you need me," Xaneth said with a cocky grin.

The last thing Eoghan wanted was to bring the arrogant Fae anywhere with them, but he would do whatever it took to get Thea back.

"It'll take all of us," Cael said.

Eoghan turned to his friend and shook his head. "Go help Rhi."

"Daire and Fintan can do that. I'll be with you, old friend."

Eoghan smiled, grateful for the friendship. He looked out at this team. "Usaeil could be anywhere. We've no id—"

His words halted as he heard his name whispered in his mind. It was faint. So very soft, he nearly missed it. But he recognized Thea's voice.

"Eoghan?" Dubhan called.

He was about to reply when he heard the music. It wasn't a violin, but it was Thea's song. He recalled the same melody she'd played at the pyramids.

"I hear her," Eoghan told the others. "Her music guides me once more."

"Thea's violin is here," Torin said.

Eoghan smiled. "She's a Halfling who has learned to play without an instrument."

"Where is she?" Cael asked. "You lead. We'll follow."

Eoghan pointed at Xaneth. "Aisling, stay with him and keep him close."

Without another word, Eoghan teleported toward the music. He made several stops before he realized that Thea was being held in the Light Castle. He relayed the information to the others when the music suddenly halted.

He immediately teleported to the castle, stopping in an empty corridor to get his bearings and determine where Thea might be. Before he could teleport again, Xaneth tackled him to the ground. Eoghan rolled the Fae onto his back and reared back his hand to punch him.

"Veil yourself," Cael said in a harsh whisper.

Eoghan looked up, recalling they were in the castle. His gaze lowered to Xaneth, who raised a brow and waited. Eoghan blew out a breath and veiled himself as he got to his feet.

Aisling stalked to Xaneth and yanked him to his feet, her veil enveloping him once they touched.

"The music stopped," Eoghan said.

Xaneth asked, "What direction was it coming from?"

Eoghan closed his eyes and tried to remember. A few seconds later, he pointed to the left.

"Usaeil must have taken Thea to her part of the castle," Xaneth said.

Aisling pulled a knife from her sleeve and put it to Xaneth's throat. "Take us there."

"Why?" he demanded. "What are you going to do? You've basically admitted that you can't kill Usaeil without Death's judgment. How do you think you're going to get Thea away from her?"

Eoghan still struggled with the fact that the music had stopped so suddenly. Thea's music. He had to find her. As long as Usaeil hadn't harmed her, then he would leave Thea with her mother—if that was what Thea wanted.

He looked around at his Reapers. Erith had been correct in saying they would be a great team. In the little time he'd been with them, Eoghan saw how they'd come together to fight as a cohesive unit.

His gaze turned to Cael. The two of them had seen much together in the eons they had been friends and brothers. They stood side by side against Bran—and after.

"I won't talk you out of it," Cael said.

Rordan raised his brows. "Wait. What?" His head swung to Eoghan. "You know where you go, we follow."

"Not this time," Eoghan told them.

Aisley pulled Xaneth after her as she walked to Eoghan. "Rordan's right. You're our leader. We follow you."

Eoghan briefly closed his eyes and inhaled deeply. "I don't know what awaits me, but if I have to battle Usaeil, I'll do it alone. I won't take the rest of you down with me."

"You assume you'll fail," Dubhan said.

Eoghan turned to Cael. "There's a reason Death judges kings, queens, and other leaders differently. We've taken them down before, so it can be done."

"He's right," Cael said. "I'd also like to point out that there's a reason Death hasn't judged Usaeil yet. We don't know what that is."

Torin swiped his hand over his chin. "I'd like to know the reason."

"We're not discussing this now," Eoghan said. "We're veiled, but anyone could hear us speaking. You all need to leave."

Cathal spread his legs and simply said, "I go where my commander goes. I'm not leaving you, Eoghan."

"Same for me," Aisling stated.

One by one, Rordan, Bradach, Dubhan, and Torin agreed.

"Don't bother trying to change their minds," Cael said. "They're yours now. You've earned their loyalty. Now, they're showing you."

Eoghan looked to Xaneth. "I gave you my word that I'd speak to Death on your behalf. If I die, one of the others will do it in my stead."

Xaneth frowned. "I thought I was coming with you."

"You're not a Reaper," Bradach said.

Xaneth smiled and said, "Ah, but you could use another fighter. And I've shown you my power. Besides, I've waited for this opportunity my entire life."

Aisling shrugged as she looked at Eoghan. "He did give us the information, and if all he said is true, then if anyone deserves to try and take out Usaeil, it's him."

"And if he dies, then none of us have to try and convince Death he should live," Rordan said.

Xaneth turned to Rordan, his gaze shooting daggers. "I love you, too."

"Enough," Eoghan said to get everyone's attention. "Everyone is going in veiled except me. Xaneth, I suppose there's a back way into the queen's chambers?"

"Oh, yeah."

"Good. Aisling. . . ." Eoghan began.

She gave a nod. "I'll see Xaneth brought there before I join the rest of you."

Eoghan then looked to Cael.

Cael shook his head. "Don't you dare tell me to leave."

"I know if the positions were reversed, that I'd stand beside you through anything. I just wanted to say thank you in case I'm not able to later."

Cael clapped him on the shoulder and squeezed. "We still have Bran to take down. I need you and your team for that, so don't even think of letting Usaeil win."

"I just want to find Thea. Alive."

Cathal withdrew his sword. "Then what are we waiting for?"

Eoghan gave a nod as everyone teleported to his or her place. He hesitated with his mind full of Thea. He held onto the hope that she was alive. Because if she weren't. . . .

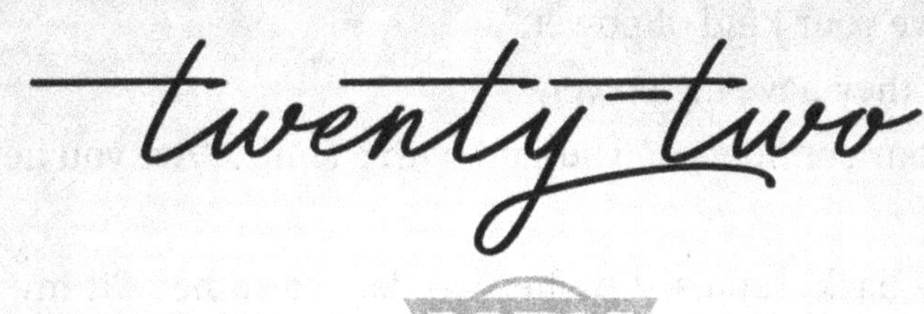

twenty-two

"No matter what, remain calm."

Cael's words rang in Eoghan's head seconds before he appeared in the massive room that made his stomach clench with dread.

The first thing Eoghan saw was Usaeil looking out the window. His gaze quickly scanned the chamber for Thea. When he saw her sprawled on the floor unmoving, he felt a bellow rise up within him.

The frenzied rage that grew quickly turned to ice as he turned to the cause of his beloved's demise. His calmness startled him, but he welcomed it.

Later, he'd allow himself to mourn what could have been.

He dropped his veil and glared at Usaeil's back for a long minute until her head jerked to the side when she realized she wasn't alone. Then, she slowly faced him.

"Who are you?" she demanded. "No one can teleport within my castle. And especially not my rooms."

He drew in a breath. "Does it frighten you to know you're not all-powerful? That someone can get through your defenses?"

She regarded him with shrewd eyes. "I'm always informed of Fae who have your kind of power."

"I doubt they have my power."

"I like your confidence," she said with a smile. "Are you here to woo me?"

He drew back, repulsed by her words. "I'd rather slit my own throat than even consider taking you to my bed."

Usaeil quickly formed a large bubble of magic and threw it at him. Eoghan didn't move. He never took his eyes off her as he waited for the orb to reach him before diverting it across the room.

The queen's eyes widened as she saw her magic slam into a wall and burn through it. She jerked her gaze to him. "You shouldn't have been able to do that."

"What kind of monarch kills her own children?" he inquired. "I believe it's the insane kind, the kind who have no business being in a seat of power."

She looked at the ceiling and shrugged while grinning. "A few have dared to try and take my throne. It didn't work out well for them. And while you do have considerably more power than they did, you'll still die."

"Will you kill me as you did Thea? Or will you send Trackers to do it for you?"

A door to Eoghan's right opened. Xaneth grinned as he walked through it, his silver eyes filled with vengeance. "By the surprise on your face, aunt, you didn't expect to see me again."

"You can't be here," she said in a shocked tone. "You're banished."

Xaneth wrinkled his nose. "If you only knew how many times I've walked these halls and brushed past your shoulders. Your

Trackers should've done a better job of killing all of us. All I wanted was to be back among my people. I'd have been content with that. I didn't want the throne, which, by the way, was never meant to be yours."

"You will die this day, Xaneth," Usaeil declared.

He laughed and spread his arms. "Come and get me. But think for just a second how I could've gotten into the castle. How we could've gotten into your castle and into your private wing without anyone seeing us."

The Reapers and Cael were stationed in a semi-circle behind Eoghan but remained veiled. They would only reveal themselves if they were needed.

While Eoghan didn't exactly appreciate Xaneth all but telling the queen they were special, Eoghan did like the fear he saw in her eyes.

Usaeil swung her gaze back to him. "Who are you?"

"A hunter, of sorts," he answered.

She backed up a step, her hands visibly shaking as she reached for the window behind her. "Reaper."

Eoghan neither confirmed nor denied it, which only made things worse for the queen. She shook her head, looking between him and Xaneth.

"No," she whispered.

Eoghan raised a brow. "No?"

"You won't take me."

He smiled then. "Is that a dare?"

She nervously licked her lips. "I won't fight you."

"Afraid?" Eoghan asked as he walked toward her.

Usaeil shrank against the wall. "I've done nothing to warrant your visit."

"Look what you've done to my cousin!" Xaneth shouted and

pointed to Thea. "What about my great-grandfather? What about the rest of my family? My baby sister!"

Eoghan held out a hand and stopped Xaneth before he could get to Usaeil.

The queen's face was pale, but she pushed away from the wall and stood tall. "The Light are a great race because of me. I joined forces with the Dragon Kings to end the Fae Wars. I've been benevolent and giving."

"You're worse than the King of the Dark," Eoghan replied.

She shot him a taciturn smile. "You want me, you'll have to catch me first."

Eoghan went to follow Usaeil after she'd teleported away, but another form appeared before him. He looked into the lavender eyes of Erith and stopped short.

"Let the queen go," Death ordered. "Her time is coming, but it isn't now."

"You've got to be kidding," Xaneth stated, fury dripping from his words.

The Reapers dropped their veils, and Aisling hastily yanked Xaneth behind her.

But Erith's attention was already on him. "I never joke, Xaneth. I know all that Usaeil has done to your family and to you. I know how many of her own children she's murdered before they could even be born. I know what she has done to Rhi, Balladyn, and countless other Fae. Believe me when I say the price she'll pay will match her crimes."

Xaneth frowned as he glanced at the others. "Who are you?"

"Death."

The Fae put his hands up, his expression instantly contrite. "I meant no disrespect."

"Yes, you did," Erith interrupted him. "I'm allowing you to live only because you helped my Reapers. And because you've known of them for months and didn't tell anyone. If, however, you had joined Bran, this conversation would've been vastly different."

Eoghan turned to Thea. Rordan and Cathal stood on either side of her like guards. Eoghan wanted to go to her, to hold her. But if he felt her lifeless body, then he'd have to accept that she was gone—and he couldn't do that.

He'd come back from losing his son with Thea's help. Who would aid him now?

Erith came to stand beside him. "She is Usaeil's child."

Eoghan turned his head to Death. "Why do you tell me this?"

"Despite Usaeil's crimes, her magic is vast and powerful."

When he frowned, Death jerked her chin to Thea. His heart missed a beat at her implication. He rushed to Thea, sliding onto his knees to stop before her.

He moved a lock of her now pale brown hair from her face and touched her cheek. Her skin was warm. When he put his finger beneath her nose, he felt her breath.

"Music is her gift," Erith said. "Whether she recognized it or not, by giving into the melody within her as Usaeil choked her, the music saved her. Just as it led you out of the other realm, Eoghan, and brought you to her when Xaneth kidnapped her, it is what prevented her death."

Eoghan gently lifted Thea in his arms and began to hum the tune he'd heard earlier that led him to the castle. The more he hummed, the more color he saw fill her skin and the more her breathing become stronger.

He wanted to shout with joy when her eyes opened, and she looked up at him.

"Hello, beautiful," he said.

She smiled and cupped his cheek. "I heard you singing."

"I thought I lost you."

Her smile melted away. "Usaeil has done horrible things."

"I know," he stopped her. "But she's gone and won't bother you again. She believes you dead."

Thea turned her head to see the others. Eoghan helped her to her feet as she went to each of them to thank them for coming for her.

Thea stopped before Cael and held out her hand. "I'm Thea."

"I'm pleased to meet you. I'm Cael," he said and bowed his head as he took her hand.

Her eyes widened in surprise. "I've heard much about you. I'm delighted to meet you. Your friendship means a great deal to Eoghan."

Eoghan clasped his hands behind his back, grinning like a fool as Cael looked his way.

"And his friendship means just as much to me," Cael replied.

Thea rubbed her throat. There was no pain any longer, but she still recalled the feeling of her larynx breaking. It wasn't something she was likely to forget.

She turned from Cael to the petite figure that stood not far from where Usaeil had earlier. The woman had thick, blue-black hair that fell down her back in waves. She was in a black, strapless gown with a tulle skirt that had yellow and red daisies sewn along the hem.

Without having to be told, Thea knew the woman was someone of great importance. Perhaps it was the way she stood so still or the way her lavender eyes commanded with simply a look.

Thea looked over her shoulder at Eoghan to find him carefully watching the stranger. Thea turned back to the woman, looking at her as Eoghan was.

That's when it dawned on Thea who she was standing before.

"You're Death," she said.

The woman smiled softly. "If it weren't for you, Eoghan would still be trapped in that other world. You drew him back to us and gave us an advantage over our enemy."

"I didn't know what I was doing," Thea said. Then she smiled as she thought of Eoghan. "But I'm glad I did."

Death looked over Thea's shoulder before meeting her gaze. "I'm aware that Eoghan told you the story of Bran."

"I know why you made the rules. They make sense."

There was a tension throughout the room that hadn't been there moments before. Thea swallowed, wondering if she had said the wrong thing.

Death took a deep breath. "There are Reapers who found love and have been allowed to stay with their women because of special circumstances involving those Halflings, or Fae in Neve's case."

Thea fought against the wave of anguish Death's words delivered. "I understand."

"I don't think you do," Death said. "I owe you a debt, my dear. You saved Eoghan. You get to choose how I repay that."

Thea turned to the side and looked at Eoghan. He shot her a wink, which made her stomach flutter in excitement.

"I think my time here is done," Cael said with a grin in Eoghan's direction. He then winked at Thea before giving a polite, if a bit cold, nod to Death before vanishing.

The other Reapers and Xaneth each bowed their heads to Death and left until all that remained was Eoghan, Thea, and Death.

"I love you," Eoghan said as he took a step toward her.

Thea nearly burst into tears right then. She blinked through them and rushed into his arms, their lips meeting in a frenzy of passion and need.

"I love you. I love you," she said between kisses.

Eoghan grasped her face between his hands. She gazed into his mercurial eyes and sighed in contentment.

"I want you," he said. "But you should know that things with Bran could go badly. There's no guarantee we'll win, or that I'll live through it."

Thea smiled and said, "I don't care. I'll take as many hours and days with you as I can get."

"I suppose that means you've chosen what you want?" Death said.

Thea and Eoghan turned to her as one. "Yes," Thea answered. "I want to be with Eoghan."

"Then so you shall," Death replied with a smile. "I wish you two much happiness."

"As I wish upon you," Eoghan said.

Death held his gaze for a moment, a deep sadness coming over her features before she disappeared.

"What was that about?" Thea asked.

Eoghan wrapped his arms around her. "I can tell you, or I can kiss you."

"Tell me later. Kiss me now."

CHAPTER
twenty-three

The sky was filled with dark clouds that already drizzled rain. Thea lifted her face upward to let the drops land on her face.

"You have to stop that," Eoghan murmured from behind her. "It makes me want to kiss you."

She smiled as she turned to face him. "I'm only looking at the rain."

"Haven't you realized that everything you do makes me crave you?"

Thea rose up on her toes and gave him a quick kiss. "This is the first time I've left your bed in two days. Annie will kill us if we don't meet her."

Eoghan flattened his lips even as he pulled her tightly against him. He moved his past her into the crowded streets of Dublin. "She's late."

"Annie will be late to her own funeral."

He grunted and turned them sideways so others wouldn't hit

her. Thea rested her head on his chest, unable to contain her smile. The last few days were delightful. But now they were over. A war was upon them, with an enemy that grew ever stronger day by day.

Death had given them a respite, of which Thea would forever be grateful. She wondered if she would ever see the stunning woman who embodied Death again.

While Thea embraced her new life with Eoghan, she knew it wasn't without dangers. Even now, the Reapers were around them. Some were veiled, while others were never far from Eoghan—though they weren't there to protect him. Eoghan could take care of himself.

The Reapers were there as a team. A unit that grew closer every day. Thea saw it with her own eyes. Walls were coming down as each of them allowed themselves to not only trust the others but also think of each other as a family.

Amazingly, they had quickly accepted her. She was thankful that Aisling was there. Otherwise, Thea might drown in all the testosterone.

Thea's eyes opened when she felt Eoghan's body stiffen slightly. She raised her head and followed his gaze to find Xaneth a few steps behind Annie.

"What is he doing here?" Eoghan mumbled.

Thea patted his chest and said, "Go ask."

"Aye."

Eoghan walked away just as Annie strode up. Her friend tried to say hello to him, but Eoghan's attention was elsewhere.

"What was that?" Annie asked in confusion.

Thea held out her arms. "It's so good to see you!"

Annie immediately hugged her, forgetting the question. She pulled back and tugged at Thea's natural brown locks before she said, "Let me look at you. My God, I didn't think it was possible for you to get more beautiful, but I think you have. Love looks good on you, girl."

Thea laughed at the sparkle in Annie's eyes. "Is it that obvious?"

"Yes," Annie said, her face showing her disgust. It was wiped away quickly. "Not that I'm not happy for you. If anyone deserves it, it's you."

"And you."

Annie shook her head. "No way. Men are good for sex, but I don't really even need them for that."

"I thought you and Noah might—"

"Not going to happen," Annie interrupted. "When you took the time off, the band fell apart."

Thea's mouth fell open. "What? I don't understand. They were together for over a year before I joined."

"The crowds didn't turn out without you. The guys started fighting until they weren't speaking to each other. I agreed to go out with Noah, and then I found him banging some girl after one of the shows."

"I'm so sorry." Thea didn't know what else to say.

Her friend waved away her words. "I quit working with the band a few days ago. I've had some others try to recruit me in the past, so I'm going to take a look at them. Or, I may do something else entirely. What about you? Other than the hunk you're with."

Thea laughed and found her gaze moving to Eoghan. Xaneth was gone, but Eoghan was now talking to Rordan. Thea returned her attention to Annie. "I'm not sure what's coming next, but I'll be with Eoghan."

"I figured," Annie said, forcing a smile. "Will you try to stay in touch though? I mean, really try?"

"I promise."

Annie swallowed as she nodded her head. "Good."

"And you'll do the same?" Thea asked.

"You know me. I'll pester you until you let me know you're alive."

Thea smiled. "You're a good friend."

"Then perhaps you'll tell your good friend what's happened over the past few days since you disappeared."

Thea glanced around. "I found out who my mother is."

Annie's blue eyes widened in surprise. "No way! How did it go? Was it wonderful or awkward?"

"It was horrible. She's the one who had me kidnapped."

"And hunky over there saved you," Annie said as she glanced at Eoghan.

Thea couldn't help but grin as she met Eoghan's gaze. "Yes, he did."

"The two of you make me want to gag. Now, back to mommy dearest."

The reminder made Thea wince. "She was awful. I hope I never see her again."

"So, as bad as the children's home was, it was better than being raised by her?" Annie asked.

"Without a doubt."

"Wow."

Thea wrinkled her nose. "Oh, yeah."

"That calls for a drink."

"I was hoping you'd say that." Thea turned toward the nearest pub. "I have a table waiting."

Eoghan watched Thea and Annie walk into the pub with Aisling and Bradach veiled and following them.

"What now?" Rordan asked.

"Xaneth didn't have to tell us anything about the Fae." Eoghan ran his hand down his face. "I doubt it's a trap, but be prepared either way."

"You want me to check it out?"

"Unless you've no interest."

Rordan's silver eyes grew intense. "I'd like nothing more than to find this Fae Xaneth mentioned. He could be of interest. Or it could be nothing."

"Take Cathal with you. I don't want you going alone."

Eoghan watched the Reaper walk away. No one had heard from Erith since her surprise appearance at the Light Castle. Robins continued to deliver names of those who had been judged, but no matter how many times Eoghan tried to contact Death, there was no answer. For Cael either.

As long as the birds brought those names, Eoghan would hold out hope that Erith was still well. But how much longer could that continue? How long until Bran either drained her of all her power, or the Reapers somehow found an advantage and killed Bran?

Eoghan ignored the rain as it began to fall harder. As long as he was alive, and as long as he was able, he would lead his team and fight for Death.

He made his way to the tavern and walked inside to where Thea and Annie awaited him. The women were laughing and had already finished half of their drinks.

His gaze was locked on Thea as he moved to her. When he neared, she rose and met him with a kiss.

"If you're going to sit with us, you can't do that," Annie told him.

He quirked a brow at her. "Averse to displays of affection?"

"Only when I know it's real, and I then I can't proclaim that love is a sham as I usually do," she said. Her lips curved into a smile. "Sit, Eoghan. I owe you for finding Thea and keeping her safe."

The three raised their glasses, clinking them together before drinking. Eoghan lowered himself beside Thea and looked at her in amazement.

Somehow, through the suffering and death, through eons of time while carrying the weight of the past, he'd found his way to something spectacular.

Thea met his gaze and smiled. Their love had been stated several times—and they would continue to do so. But it was also in every look, every word, and every touch they shared.

For they were joined now and forever.

"Oh, bloody hell. When's the damn wedding?" Annie grumbled.

Eoghan grinned and raised a brow in question to Thea.

"Is now too soon?" Thea asked.

Annie let out a loud moan and dropped her head back for a moment. "Have I taught you nothing? You need to plan."

Thea shrugged. "I think our hearts have already said it all."

"Aye," Eoghan agreed.

Annie looked away with a loud sigh. "I don't think I can be around the two of you."

Eoghan shared a laugh with Thea as they linked hands. Their hearts and souls were already connected, but Eoghan would happily say the words if that's what Thea wanted and needed.

Because he couldn't imagine a day without her. She was his, the music of his spirit, the one who'd saved him from the darkness and gave him life.

Epilogue

The beautiful O'Byrne land was now destroyed. When Erith hid her sword deep beneath the soil, she'd never once thought that there would come a time when she would need it again.

But she was back.

She didn't know if Seamus had learned anything from Bran yet. For all she knew, the Dark Fae had turned on her. But she didn't think so. In the time she'd held Seamus in her realm, she had come to know him well.

If he were born to the Light instead of the Dark, his life would have turned out much differently. He truly regretted accidentally freeing Bran. In an attempt to make up for it, Seamus was going to spy for her. It might very well end the Fae's life.

Erith didn't bother to veil herself as she walked across the land. None of Bran's men could kill her. Yet. And Bran was occupied elsewhere for the moment.

She walked through the rubble that was the O'Byrne home and

regretted what had befallen Ettie and her sisters. Erith had sworn never to pick up her sword again, not after the havoc she'd wrought during that period of her life.

It wasn't in her nature to sit back and allow her life and magic to be drained from her, but she was nearly to the point where it no longer mattered. She'd waited too long to come to her senses and want to fight.

Mostly because she feared what holding the sword would do to her.

Again.

But if she didn't, she would die. Her Reapers and allies would be slaughtered. The mortals would be enslaved, and there was no telling what would become of the Fae.

This was no longer just about her. It was about everything—and everyone—else.

She halted and briefly closed her eyes as she prepared herself for what was about to happen. Several millennia had passed since she'd last wielded the sword, but she could still recall the power that ran through the black metal and into her hand.

Would she be strong enough to return the sword to the ground once she ended Bran? She really hoped she was.

Erith opened her eyes and held out her palm over the field. The earth shook and trembled beneath her feet before the weapon shot up from the ground.

Her fingers wrapped around the hilt, catching it.

Cael hadn't known what had brought him back to Killarney until he spotted Erith slowly walking the land, the hem of her black skirts getting muddy from the recent rain.

She didn't notice him despite the fact that he wasn't veiled. Her attention seemed to be elsewhere. He didn't approach her. Instead, he remained at a distance, watching.

It wasn't long before she stopped and held out her hand. He frowned when the ground started to shake, and then the black sword Ettie had wielded against Bran—the very weapon Bran had wrecked the land searching for—flew straight into Erith's hand.

Cael took a step back when her eyes briefly glowed. His mouth fell open when the ball gown she usually wore was replaced by a short, chainmail shirt covered in strips of black leather and a leather breastplate. Then that too faded when the ball gown returned.

A gust of wind suddenly whipped through the glade and swirled around Death, lifting her blue-black locks and her skirt.

Her head swiveled to him, their gazes locking. Then, she was gone.

Cael stared at the now-empty spot for several minutes, trying to comprehend what he'd just seen. There was no mistaking the weapon. Erith was finally going after Bran.

Thank you for reading **DARK ALPHA'S HUNGER**.
I hope you enjoyed the story as much as I loved writing it.

If you want more Reapers, then you're in luck!
Up next is **DARK ALPHA'S AWAKENING**.

BUY DARK ALPHA'S AWAKENING NOW
at www.DonnaGrant.com

◆

And don't miss out on the Dark Kings series.
The next book set in Dark Universe, is **DRAGON NIGHT**...

BUY DRAGON NIGHT NOW
at www.DonnaGrant.com

◆

To find out when new books release
SIGN UP FOR MY NEWSLETTER today at
https://www.tinyurl.com/DonnaGrantNews

Join my Facebook group, Donna Grant Groupies, for exclusive
giveaways and sneak peeks of future books.
https://bit.ly/DGGroupies

◆

Keep reading for a peek of DARK ALPHA'S AWAKENING and a
glimpse at DRAGON NIGHT ...

SNEAK PEEK AT DARK ALPHA'S AWAKENING

REAPER SERIES, BOOK 7

There is no escaping a Reaper. I am an elite assassin, part of a brotherhood that only answers to Death. And when Death says your time is up, I'm coming for you...

Serving Death and the Reapers has been my life for centuries. I've always put my duty before everything, even my yearning for Death. But now, she's fading – our foe is bent on destroying her and he will stop at nothing until he does. Death holds the key to our survival. I will do everything in my power to stop her from disappearing. For her, I will ensure we have the best fighting chance. For her...I will cross the divide keeping us apart.

DARK ALPHA'S AWAKENING

Excerpt

March

Inchmickery, Scotland — Reaper stronghold

He was dying. Cael didn't need to look at his wound or the blood pooling around him to know that his life was coming to an end.

Shite. Everything hurt. He leaned his head back against the fallen tree. He could hear the distant sounds of battle. How could he have been so stupid as to follow two of the weakest, most cowardly Fae into the forest without backup?

He should've known something was wrong the moment he entered the woods, but he'd been too intent on stopping them from deserting. It wasn't until the last second that he realized that had been their intent all along.

The minute the two deserters stopped and faced him, Cael had known things were about to go sideways. And had they ever. He was surrounded by Dark within seconds.

Yet, it hadn't been the Dark who killed him. It had been his men.

He coughed, blood running from the corner of his lips. With a swipe of his one useful arm, he wiped it away. His injuries would keep him immobile and dying a slow, painful demise.

Certainly not the death of a warrior.

Not the passing he'd expected for more years than he could remember.

Cael coughed again. He had to get his mind off the agony of his body. He tried to think of Corla. She had promised herself to him. He had thought he loved her. Would have sworn his heart was Corla's.

Then he beheld the woman. Even now he could recall every detail of her. He was in the middle of battle, dodging Dark orbs and using both his magic and his sword to push back the enemy. His focus had been entirely on the enemy.

And yet, for reasons that he couldn't explain even now, his head turned to the side and his gaze landed on her. Beautiful couldn't begin to describe her. She stood on the fringes of the battle, unfazed at the carnage as she stared at him – him! - with lavender eyes.

He had to know her, had to find out who she was. By the time the battle was over, she was nowhere to be found. Cael had searched the dead, fearing she had been killed. But he found no trace of her.

Yet, her image lingered in his mind. Blue-black waves of hair falling freely to her waist. And eyes that knew not only the secrets of the universe, but that had seen everything.

He wanted her heart and her body. Because in that millisecond of time, he knew he was meant to be with her.

Knowing it and finding her where two different things. Nearly a thousand years passed without a single trace of her. So much for his vow to find her. Now, he would go to his grave without knowing her name.

The sound of footsteps approaching alerted him that his torture wasn't finished. He looked to his sword. With his teeth clenched, he leaned to the side to reach for his weapon. Blood gushed from his wounds and pain sliced through him, robbing him of breath.

Sweat beaded his brow as he fought not to make a sound while he struggled to right himself again with only one hand, all while holding his sword. If he were going to die, he'd do it while holding onto his weapon.

The Dark were closing in on him again. He counted six of them. Then out of nowhere a petite figure appeared spinning and turning from one Dark to another while a sword danced as swiftly as the attacker's feet.

Cael had seen a lot of Fae fight, but he'd never seen one who moved like this. The speed was unlike anything he'd ever witnessed, but it was the way the assailant attacked that was staggering to watch.

Within seconds, the Dark were dead. All without one finger being laid upon the tiny person. They stood with their back to him, a helmet on to hide their face.

He wanted to tell them how amazing they were and thank them for the help, but he was fading fast. Cael kept his eyes on the figure as they turned. His heart missed a beat when the helmet was removed and he found himself looking into the face of the woman he'd been searching for.

The helmet and sword vanished, as did her bloodstained clothes, replaced by a long black gown with a full skirt. Her black hair was in an intricate braid.

"Hello, Cael," she said.

He had no idea how she knew his name, and it didn't matter. She was with him. He wouldn't die alone.

Cael fought to keep his eyes open. She knelt beside him and took his hand, her lavender eyes locked with his. He couldn't believe she was there and touching him. The betrayal of his men didn't matter anymore.

"I can offer you another life," she whispered.

He frowned, unsure he'd heard her correctly. Then his lids became too heavy to keep open and they closed. It became harder to breathe. He wanted to stay with her. He would endure pain for eternity just to be with her. But he no longer had any say in such matters.

Her hand flattened against the side of his face as his life faded. Seconds later, the pain left him, but he could still feel her touch. He opened his eyes to her.

"I'm Death, Cael. I'm here to offer you a position as one of my Reapers."

His eyes snapped open as he sat up in the bed. Cael couldn't remember the last time he'd thought about the day he became a Reaper. The dream had been so vivid, as if he were reliving the entire event.

He swung his legs over the side of the bed and dropped his chin to his chest. He stayed there only a few minutes before he rose and dressed.

Wind howled outside as a storm lashed the east coast of Scotland. The Reapers had been in Inchmickery for a while now. He hated being so far from Ireland, but they had to keep ahead of their enemy.

He strode through the old concrete compound that the humans abandoned years ago. His six Reapers were in residence as well. Few were up at the early hour. This was the time Cael took each morning to think about the day ahead and anything that might have gone wrong the day before.

Cael walked through the door and came to stand outside beneath a protective overhang. Waves crashed violently against the rocks and concrete, sending water soaring. The wind drove the rain at an angle, drenching everything – including him. But he didn't care.

"I suppose you're going to stand there brooding all day."

Cael drew in a breath at the sound of Fintan's voice. Once one of the most feared – and infamous – assassins of the Fae, Fintan was an integral part of the Reapers.

A group Cael led.

"What is it?" Fintan asked over the sound of the storm.

Cael waited until Fintan was even with him. "Do you remember when you became a Reaper?"

"I do. It's not exactly something you forget."

"I suppose not."

Fintan crossed his arms over his chest, uncaring that the waves drenched him. "Spit it out, Cael. What's bothering you?"

Cael had come out to be alone. It seemed fitting that there was a storm since he'd felt one within himself for some time. He looked into Fintan's red-rimmed white eyes. "I dreamed of the day I became a Reaper."

Fintan shoved his long, white hair from his face after a wave struck him. "So?" he asked, confusion marring his face.

"Have you done that?"

"No."

"Why did I?"

Fintan raised a brow. "You ask me things I can't answer."

"The dream meant something."

"About Erith?"

Cael braced himself for the wave before it hit. As leader of the Reapers, he knew how each of them had been betrayed. It was one of many gifts given to him by Death.

Death. Erith.

Her.

He'd known her by all three names. The attraction he felt for her hadn't dimmed when he discovered she was Death. In fact, it increased.

Right on the heels of that was discovering that there could never be anything between them. Not even the knowledge that he would spend eons near her but never have her could have made him refuse her offer.

Being a Reaper meant everything to him. He was doing more for the Fae now than he had when he lived among them.

"Cael?"

He swung his head to Fintan, only then realizing he had never answered. "I do think it was about Erith. It's always been about her."

"You're referring to Bran," Fintan said, his lips peeled back in a sneer.

Bran. The Reaper who had defied Death and not only fell in love, but told the Fae who he was. Both offences were grave. Cael still believed Erith would have ignored Bran's falling in love, despite her rule that there be no relationships. But Bran had broken the first rule of being a Reaper: No Fae could know who they were.

Death had no choice but to carry out her punishment to the Light Fae and end her life. Bran had gone mad with grief. He split the Reapers, forcing them to fight each other.

Cael had been the newest member of the group. He and Eoghan had bonded quickly, both of them looking up to their leader, Theo. So when Bran and the other Reapers killed Theo, there was no other option for Cael and Eoghan than to fight Bran.

Before either Cael or Eoghan could slay Bran, Erith stepped in and tossed Bran into a realm she created just for his punishment.

Who could have guessed that thousands of years later,

someone would let Bran loose? Or that Bran would somehow learn how to syphon Death's power and life force?

"We need to end him," Cael said.

Fintan snorted. "That's not something you need to convince any of us to do. We're all ready."

"There's something you don't know. I saw Death recently. She returned to the O'Byrne land."

Fintan's brow furrowed deeply. "Are you telling me she got the black sword that Ettie used? The one Bran hunted for?"

Cael nodded. "She called for it. It belongs to her. More than that, I saw her clothes change for just a moment into leather and chainmail."

"Fek me," Fintan murmured as he ran a hand down his face. "She's the Mistress of War, isn't she?"

Cael thought back to the day he saw her fight. The day he died and was reborn a Reaper. He'd known she was special before learning she was Death. "I think so."

"Why did she stop?" Fintan's surprise gave way to anger. "And why the fek hasn't she gone after Bran before now? Why has she waited? If she's the Mistress of War, there's nothing more powerful than her. She could wipe Bran out with a thought."

"Perhaps at one time, but not now," Cael reminded his friend. "Bran has taken too much of her power."

Fintan turned his back on a wave that slammed into him. "But she has the sword."

"Which means she's going after Bran."

"Not alone," Fintan stated.

Cael grinned. "No, she won't be alone. Whether she agrees or not, we'll be there with her."

"Have you told her that?"

"Not yet."

Fintan crossed his arms over his chest. "Do you know where she's at? She did refuse to answer any of us for quite some time."

"I'm not going to look for her. I'm going to look for Bran. He wants to fight me anyway, right?"

Fintan's smile was slow. "Oh, I like this plan. Shall I tell the others?"

"Aye. We need to come up with a plan."

"What about Eoghan and his Reapers?"

"We're going to need them as well." He still couldn't believe Eoghan had returned and there were more Reapers, but he was glad of it. "So far Bran doesn't know of them. Let's make certain it stays that way until it's time."

Fintan slapped him on the back. "Don't worry, brother. Bran's days are numbered."

Cael waited until Fintan returned inside before he let out a sigh. He hoped they were able to move fast enough and destroy Bran before Erith was past the point of no return.

Because a life without her wasn't a life worth living.

He said Eoghan's name and waited for his friend to arrive. It was time they had a talk.

BUY DARK ALPHA'S AWAKENING NOW
at www.DonnaGrant.com

GLIMPSE AT THE NEXT DARK UNIVERSE BOOK

DRAGON NIGHT, DARK KINGS SERIES, BOOK 9.5

Governed by honor and ruled by desire

There has never been a hunt that Dorian has lost. With his sights sent on a relic the Dragon Kings need to battle an ancient foe, he won't let anything stand in his way – especially not the beautiful owner. Alexandra is smart and cautious. Yet the attraction between them is impossible to deny – or ignore. But is it a road Dorian dares to travel down again?

With her vast family fortune, Alexandra Sheridan is never without suitors. No one is more surprised than she when the charming, devilish Scotsman snags her attention. But the secrets Dorian holds is like a wall between them until one fateful night when he shares everything. In his arms she finds passion like no other – and a love that will transcend time. But can she give her heart to a dragon?

BUY DRAGON NIGHT TODAY
at www.DonnaGrant.com

ABOUT THE AUTHOR

New York Times and *USA Today* bestselling author Donna Grant® has been praised for her "totally addictive" and "unique and sensual" stories.

She's written more than one hundred novels spanning multiple genres of romance including the bestselling Dragon Kings® series that features a thrilling combination of Druids, Fae, and immortal Highlanders who are dark, dangerous, and irresistible. She lives in Texas with her dog and a cat.

www.DonnaGrant.com
www.MotherofDragonsBooks.com

facebook.com/AuthorDonnaGrant
instagram.com/dgauthor
tiktok.com/@donnagrant_author
bookbub.com/authors/donna-grant
goodreads.com/donna_grant
pinterest.com/donnagrant1

9 781958 353837